Topically Challenged

Volume 1

Copyright © 2021 Christopher Fielden. All rights reserved.

The copyright of each story published in this anthology remains with the author.

Cover copyright © 2021 David Fielden. All rights reserved.

Alice's 'Trump This' News Writing Challenge was conceived by A.H. Creed.

Transcription and proofreading: Angela Googh

First published April 2021.

The rights of the writers of the short stories published in this anthology to be identified as the authors of their work has been asserted in accordance with the Copyright, Designs and Patents Act 1988.

All rights reserved. No part of this publication may be reproduced, stored in a retrieval system, or transmitted in any form by any means, electronic, mechanical, photocopying, recording or otherwise, without the prior permission of the publishers.

You can learn more about Alice's 'Trump This' News Writing Challenge and many other writing challenges at:

www.christopherfielden.com

All characters in this publication are fictitious and any resemblance to real persons, living or dead, is purely coincidental.

ISBN: 9798714105012

DEDICATION

This book is dedicated to the memory of Gail Wareham Everett. Gail was an active member and administrator of the Authors of the Flash Fiction Writing Challenges Facebook group and has contributed stories to many of the books published via the writing challenges. She will be deeply missed.

TOPICALLY CHALLENGED

A.H. Creed and Christopher Fielden, pictured in Cardiff whilst conceiving Alice's 'Trump This' News Writing Challenge

INTRODUCTION 1

by A.H. Creed

When not writing in my pen name – Ballpoint – I can be found down a plot hole on Writer's Block.

These one hundred micro stories, written in a time that started with Trump and ended with a pandemic, are tales of an unexpected world.

Insightful, personal and often funny takes on *The News*, they are (in journalistic phraseology) snapshots of their time.

Now, if that's not enough to make you buy this book (the profits from which make a much-needed donation to a children's reading charity) then consider this: There is a planet with clouds made of sapphires and rubies. At one thousand-ish light years away, there's no chance you'll get to go there and be rained on, but there are one hundred chances that this book cloud contains a rare, raw gem from a future bestselling author.

"Why a news challenge?" at least one person has asked. I'd like to say my precognitive powers told me we were headed for newsworthy times. But that would be a Cummings-like justification that you're not going to believe any more than my partner believes I needed to eat a whole box of chocolates to test my taste buds.

The truth is the news is a freely-available resource of random inspiration. And sometimes, it's only by writing (and thinking) on a new tangent that we can get around the walls we have built for ourselves.

Enjoy.

A.H. Creed, Cardiff, January 2021.

www.murdereader.com

INTRODUCTION 2

by Chris Fielden

When A.H. Creed approached me with her idea for a news themed challenge, I thought it had a lot of potential. So, one autumnal day in 2018, I hopped into my van and drove over the Prince of Wales Bridge to Cardiff. There, we thrashed out the idea and Alice's 'Trump This' News Writing Challenge came to life, named after some bloke no one's heard of because he hasn't been in the news very much over the last few years. Apologies for the industrial bucket of sarcasm dolloped onto the previous sentence...

The idea behind the challenge was to highlight the importance of a story's theme. When a writer is struggling to find fresh ideas, the news can be used to inspire a story and spark the imagination; it can provide a theme and help cure writer's block.

Themes are important because they can form the central focus of a story, connecting all its aspects, including the characters, plot, conflict, situation and resolution, giving a message for the reader to think about. If a theme resonates with a reader, it can help them remember a story long after they've finished it.

And so, the challenge was launched in October 2018. Early in January 2021, we received our 100th story and this book went into production. This coincided with the tenure of that bloke I mentioned earlier coming to an end.

It seemed an appropriate time to close the challenge, marking the occasion and, at the same time, making this 14th book unique within the writing challenge series. We have published 100 news themed stories and not a story more. This anthology showcases those stories, inspired by history unfolding during a small snapshot of time.

So much has happened recently, and I think it's fair to say that much of it has been endured rather than enjoyed. Therefore, it pleases me that the majority of the stories in this book focus on the positive, or simply try to tease a smile from the reader's lips. We need that now, more than ever.

I'd like to thank every writer who has submitted their work to the news challenge. And every reader who has purchased this book. You're enabling writers to have fun with words, which is what these challenges are all about.

There are 100 stories written by 100 authors in this book. It's our pleasure to present them in this one-off collection of news themed tales.

Over and out.

Chris Fielden, Portishead, January 2021.

www.christopherfielden.com

INTRODUCTION 3

by BookTrust

We are the UK's largest reading charity and reach 3.9 million children each year with books, resources and support to help children develop a reading habit.

We do this in lots of different ways, but our priority is to get more children excited about books, rhymes and stories – because if reading is fun, children will want to do it. We run nationwide programmes – like our flagship programme Bookstart. We reach millions of families across the country each year with books, resources and advice to encourage parents and carers to start reading with their babies right from the beginning.

Much of our focus is on these early years because we've learnt that starting early and involving the whole family is the best way to get children reading. We also work with schools to support teachers and school librarians to get children and young people excited about books and reading. We want all families to have access to reading, which is why we also deliver more targeted programmes aimed at helping those who need us most – whether that's families facing economic hardship, children in care or children with additional needs. We want every child to have the best possible start in life. It's why we're so passionate about getting children reading.

Thank you to everyone involved in creating this anthology and for donating funds which will go towards helping children who need additional support to get reading.

www.booktrust.org.uk

ACKNOWLEDGMENTS

Thank you to A.H. Creed for conceiving and helping me bring the news challenge to life.
www.murdereader.com

Thanks to David Fielden for designing the cover of this book and building and maintaining my website. Without him, I'd never have created a platform that allowed the writing challenges to be so successful. You can learn more about Dave's website building skills at:
www.bluetree.co.uk

Thank you to Angela Googh for her help preparing the interior of this book.

And finally, a big THANK YOU to everyone who has submitted stories, purchased anthologies, supported this newsworthy idea and, in turn, BookTrust. Without the support and generosity of all the writers who submit their stories and the readers who buy the anthologies, this simply wouldn't be possible.

TOPICALLY CHALLENGED

VOLUME 1

1: WILLPOWER

by A.H. Creed

Inspired by: "Out of their minds: wild ideas at the 'Coachella of consciousness'" by Tom Bartlett, *The Guardian*

I'd lost another job to a robot and my rent was overdue. In desperation, I called the Let Someone Else Suffer company. I was rejected because I'm dental phobic but referred to another Consciousness Exchange body-swap agency specialising in getting lazy actors into shape.

After 29 days of avoiding my body-swapper's mother's house (the dog attacked me), and making increasingly lame excuses to her frustrated boyfriend, I wished I hadn't signed up for the secrecy bonus. Over-exercised, sugar-deprived and alone, I couldn't even enjoy her penthouse luxury, and dreaded the last few days: dermabrasion, starvation and waxing.

When the super-rich super-star was back in her now super-skinny body and I was wobbling my over-indulged fatter body home, I decided, creativity being the only thing robots can't do better, to write about my experience. About the rich paying for their perfections with the suffering of the poor...

No. That wasn't news. That was repetition.

Lightbulb moment – I'd write 'What it is to be a woman', from one man's objective perspective.

A.H. Creed's Biography

I am dyslexic, I can't spell. Don't know my commas from my colon, which means I don't write well. But sometimes I write unique, and sometimes I write funny. So I might write *Sixty Shades*, and make loads of money.
www.murdereader.com

2: SOME INTEGRITY WITH YOUR CHIPS?

by Christopher Fielden

Inspired by: "One-eyed cat makes an incredible 230-mile journey from Hull to Bristol – clinging to bottom of lorry" by Stephen White, *The Daily Mirror*

"Do you have anything to say?" you ask.

"I have diplomatic immunity, at all of the times."

"Had."

A small crowd of survivors have gathered on the hilltop. They watch solemnly as the prisoner is locked into stocks beneath a guillotine's heavy blade.

"We did everything in a humane way, the very best way." In the distance, a war-torn building crumbles and a cloud of dust drifts lazily into the sky.

"If you repeat a lie often enough it becomes the truth."

"I never said that. It's not something I'd say."

"Goebbels said it."

"Who?"

Sighing, you pull back the prisoner's collar. There's a scar on his neck. "*No one* was implant exempt. One truth, at least." You press your TruthChip™ reader against his skin. It hums, beeps and displays data. Events, thoughts, actions, consequences. *Everything*.

"What you're seeing and what you're reading is not what's happening. Or what happened. It didn't happen like that." He looks old. Feeble. Spent.

You unlock the stocks. "Please, leave. Just go."

As he stumbles away, confusion on his face, birdsong caresses the breeze.

Christopher Fielden's Biography

When I conceived the To Hull And Back humorous short story competition, I never thought my 'book strapped to a motorbike' escapades would be upstaged. Sometimes, it's good to be put in one's place, especially by a one-eyed cat called Lucy.
   www.christopherfielden.com

3: AGE DOES NOT WITHER

by Sarah Mosedale

Inspired by: "102-year-old former racing driver rescued from roof after three days" by Damien Gayle, *The Guardian*

I never understood why anyone let their age get in the way. Personally, I'd become an internationally renowned limbo dancer at 65, broken the world free diving record at 72 and gracefully acknowledged receipt of three Michelin stars the day after my 93rd birthday. So when the news broke about the Scottish nuclear meltdown, I immediately set off in the Morris Minor to see what I could do.

Got the usual response, of course, but I'm pretty much immune by now. I just let them get on with their tutting and head shaking. They'd cordoned off a circle about a mile in diameter but done a lousy job as per. It was child's play to break through and the shouting soon died away behind me. The problem was easy to spot for someone like myself, who had fitted in a doctorate in nuclear physics somewhere between puberty and a brief midlife crisis. I soon had the situation under control and was heading back.

What a lot of fuss, though. All those hazmat suits and Geiger counters going crazy. Quite ridiculous.

Sarah Mosedale's Biography

Sarah Mosedale lives in Bury, Manchester, and after doing many other things, some quite interesting, is now embarking on a new life as a flash fiction writer and loving every minute of it.

4: THE MISSION OF LIFE

by Debbie Singh

Inspired by: "NASA spacecraft on mission to 'touch the sun' looks back to take shot of Earth" by Rob Waugh, *Yahoo*

Parker checked all the instruments – all correct and working, lights flashing, buttons beeping. Next, the special wide-field probing imager – check. Good, everything was ready to go. Outside, the sun loomed ever nearer. The metal exterior began to buckle and bend while red and orange streaks shimmied and shone from it, making it look as though it was part of the sun itself. The bright light was blinding and all consuming.

Seven years in the making, this had been. Seven years of preparation, of waiting, of finally being able to see the full workings of this magnificent star. Ninety-three million miles to fly right into its corona. It always was a one-way mission, Parker knew that, but the knowledge this mission would give would be priceless.

'Parker Solar Probe to NASA. Images and data being transmitted now. Please respond.'

The message crossed space before Parker crashed. Back on Earth, nobody received the message. The devastation of nuclear war had erased the very men who had created the probe and left the world in darkness.

Debbie Singh's Biography

I live in London and at the moment am a part time student. I haven't had any formal training with writing, it's more a hobby. I thought I'd give it a try and send in a short story.

5: SUGAR AND DOUGHNUTS

by Derek McMillan

Inspired by: "The Apprentice 2018: Who left The Apprentice last night?" by Samuel Spencer, *Express*

"Lord Sugar will see you now."

Two thoughts went through my mind as I did the walk of shame. One was, *Why is a high-flier like myself being called back into the boardroom to face the possible attack of Sugar's sacking finger?* The other was, *Who wants to work for a bully anyway?*

"You've been a ruddy disgrace in this task. All you had to do was bake some ruddy doughnuts and you couldn't even do that."

"I've never baked a doughnut before."

"I'll tell you what. I'm looking at a load of doughnuts now." The audience tittered obediently. "So what I want to know is, who else are you bringing back into the boardroom with you?"

"Nobody."

"That's not how this process works. You have to have someone else in your team to blame."

"No. The team worked well. I was the PM. I should go."

"Well, have it your own way, Mr Smartypants." The deadly finger pointed. "You're fired."

"Thank you for the opportunity, Lord Vader."

"Can't even get my ruddy name right."

I was free.

Derek McMillan's Biography

Derek McMillan lives in Durrington with his wife, Angela, who is also his editor. His latest book is *Durrington Detective Agency,* which is a collection of short detective stories with something for everybody.

6: DOG'S DAY OUT

by Hullabaloo22

Inspired by: "#dogsatpollingstations trends on Twitter as pooches visit the polls" by Anonymous, *The Irish Times*

"Mum, come on. You wanted to vote before school, remember."

"Oh, that's changed, Sylvie. I'll drop you off and pop down to vote later."

The drive to school was perhaps a bit speedier than normal. Sylvie climbed out of the car, paused to say goodbye, then gave up as her mother seemed deep in conversation with another parent.

Back home, Helen ran the bath, collected the towels and the special shampoo, finally calling out, "Sugarpuff."

The West Highland Terrier had been listening and had no intention of answering that call. Escape was impossible and the small white dog soon found herself in hot water, shampoo suds threatening her eyes.

Sugarpuff did get in a good shake before the rest of the grooming took place and she found herself bundled into the car.

Outside the polling booth, parents were gathered, phones at the ready and pooches on show. Snap and upload – look where we are. The fact that voting cards remained at home was overlooked; at least they could prove that they had turned up at the polling station.

Hullabaloo22's Biography

Hullabaloo22 lives in the South West of Ireland. She writes in a multitude of genres and is a frequent poster to *Booksie.com*. She has had short stories and poems published in volumes 3 and 4 of *The Ronin Express*.

7: BEYOND OUR LIMITS

by Sandra Orellana

Inspired by: "The migrant caravan could be weeks away from the US border" by Catherine E. Shoichet, Natalie Gallón and Patrick Oppmann, *CNN*

"Why are you crying?" Tommy asked a young, poorly dressed boy.

"I live on the other side of the border. Because we're a country with no money, your leader makes us feel helpless. Is it how I dress? The colour of my face? Is it my fault we're not important?"

Tommy listened and put his hand on the boy's shoulder. He said, "Be brave, my friend."

Tommy remembered his father taught him to love and live in harmony with his neighbour, for the sake of the border. He'd watched how the people listened to the leader of his country.

He looked at the boy, and said, "We will meet again. Strangers we will never be. We will fight against him trying to divide us. Even if we have to go beyond, by travelling through the clouds, we'll meet again. This wall will not be built. It won't give us peace. Our generation will prevail."

Tommy saw the boy smile up at him, eyes full of hope. "Thank you, my friend. We will meet again."

Sandra Orellana's Biography

Sandra Orellana, 64, American, living in Mexico. Passions are tennis and writing. Reaches out to shelters. Her first novel available on Amazon, *The Arch of Surprises*. Her children's book will launch soon. Working on her second novel. Enjoys Christopher's challenges.

8: YOU HAVE REACHED YOUR DESTINATION

by Frank Havemann

Inspired by: "Air pollution is the 'new tobacco', warns WHO head" by Anonymous, *The Guardian*

Air pollution is the new tobacco. The headline has been bouncing around her head since breakfast. Her lungs ache as she cycles through the traffic along Marylebone Road, the sour taste of diesel on her tongue. It's her third delivery of the day, and she needs to pick up the pace if she wants to make rent *and* have a social life this month.

Three years of Chemistry at Imperial haven't quite worked out, yet. The handful of bio-tech start-ups she has oscillated between ranged from millennial coffee clubs to half-hearted get-rich-quick schemes.

"You have reached your destination," chirps her phone. She dashes past freezing smokers, savouring their poison, grinning widely.

The cocktail glasses chime gently as a waiter attends to the murmuring guests. She takes a few slow breaths before stepping up to the microphone. "Ladies and gentlemen, thank you for funding Breathe London, and welcome to our first shareholder celebration." The condenser-collectors are installed along the main roads and she has found a cheap manufacturer for the inhalers. Every crisis is an opportunity.

Frank Havemann's Biography

Frank Havemann is from the 80's and lives in Oxford, UK, with his family and cats, enjoying a rich diet of writing, maths, books, gardening, photography, music and sports.

9: WASTE NOT, WANT NOT

by Barbara Hull

Inspired by: "Parisian mayor launches 'rat map' to tackle rodent menace" by Kim Willsher, *The Guardian*

I really wanted to impress her when she came to see me in Paris.

"We're going to Chez Paul for lunch."

"What's that?"

"Trendiest place in Paris, just opened."

"What nationality is it? French?"

"Not sure. A lot of the menu's in Latin but you'll see, it's really delicious."

I had reserved a table, otherwise we wouldn't get in. The entrée was fairly simple, crudités variées and oeuf dur mayonnaise.

There was a choice of main course: Cavia porcellus au vin, Escalope Norvegicus, Fricassé de Myocastor, Blanquette de Mus.

"What do you recommend?" she asked the waiter.

"The Escalope Norvegicus is by far our most popular dish."

So that's what we had, followed by a very respectable Tarte Tatin with Crème Chantilly.

On the way back to my flat, she said, "I've been reading about the problem of sewer rats in Paris. Have you seen any?"

"Oh, I think it's just paper talk."

I had just found on my mobile, 'Norvegicus, the brown rat, also known as the common rat, street rat, sewer rat, Hanover rat, Norwegian rat, Parisian rat...'

Barbara Hull's Biography

Barbara Hull is a retired lecturer, originally a Mancunian but now living in York. Passionate about languages, she is an avid reader, especially in Italian and French. She is a champion of Adult and Continuing Education.

10: STRAWBERRY FIELDS ARE NOT FOREVER

by Kelly Van Nelson

Inspired by: "'Food terrorism' and other possible culprits behind the strawberry contamination scare" by Hagar Cohen and David Lewis, *ABC News*

Australian strawberry crops attacked by fundamentalists using weapons of mass destruction.

Sewing needles use pointed approaches to eradicate freedom. In brutal acts of genocide, contaminated strawberries have been tossed into landfills, stripped of basic rights to live a fruitful life. Australia regrets not implementing a Declaration of Independence. Liberal Party lottery winner, Morrison, is obtaining advice from Trump around building walls to keep out unwanted illegal immigrants. Australia must protect homeland soil from this spreading epidemic to avoid it going pear-shaped. Food terrorism is not funny, unless writing about it. Then it's all about the pun...net.

Protecting their berry existence from deeply-rooted radicalisation is challenging and survival short-lived. Freedom-fighters passing through shoe bomber metal detectors, are:

- Boiled until sewing needles are in a jam.
- Consumed in champagne – alcohol poisoning beats becoming a pin cushion.
- Sweetened with sugar and cream. Wimbledon does everything white.
- Blended with yogurt. Likelihood of Nutri-Bullet damage slimmer than smoothie-drinking health-freaks.

Vigilantes looking for a needle in a strawberry stack,

rest assured, an eye is on these needles. Justice will prevail. This is not the last straw.

Kelly Van Nelson's Biography

Kelly Van Nelson is a fiction author represented by The Newman Agency, with several short stories, poems and magazine articles published in the UK, USA and Australia. Novel shortlisted PenFro, longlisted Exeter Novel Prize, third place Yeovil Literary Prize.

www.kellyvannelson.com

11: THAT'S OK THEN

by Ken Frape

Inspired by: "Bristol university suicides spark mental health alerts" by Anonymous, *BBC*

"Another student suicide," reports regional news programme. "Victim depressed, not drunk." Same outcome though.

University states, "More money than ever before, in real terms, going into student welfare."

"That's OK then," says stand-up comedian at university gig.

"Student debt climbing," says think tank. "Now averages £57,000."

"Can't put a price on a university education," says Universities Minister.

"Yes you can," says NUS. "It averages out at £57,000 per student."

Another student suicide. Was worried about job prospects in post-Brexit Britain, in the event of a no-deal scenario and £57,000 in debt.

"I am determined to negotiate a good deal for the country with more jobs," says PM. "We are not contemplating a no-deal Brexit."

"That's OK then," says stand-up comedian at university gig.

Another student suicide. Worried about the state of the world, with unstable leaders threatening Armageddon.

Government spokesperson says, "The student suicide rate has decreased by 27% during the past 12 months, indicating that ongoing investment and

Government policies are having a positive effect."

"That's OK then," says stand-up comedian at university gig.

Meanwhile, another student suicide...

Ken Frape's Biography

Ken Frape has been writing stuff, like short stories, letters, plays and flash fiction for only a short time. He says he is still learning. Several short stories and flash fiction have been published in anthologies and the like.

12: STONED

by Cathy Cade

Inspired by: "Bungling robbers ram-raided a village Co-Op with a TRACTOR only to flee empty handed when they knocked down most of the shop" by Amie Gordon, *Mail Online*

"Jump in, Timbo. Keys were in barn."

"You were meant to wait. You nearly mowed me down."

"Well, I hadn't found brake, had I?"

"Are you drunk?"

"Nah. Just a li'l celebration. 'S my first time driving a tractor."

Pause. "Nobby said you lived on a farm."

"'Assright. My girlfriend's renting a converted barn."

"Right... Nobby's texted. He's nicked a getaway car and he's waiting for us. Turn off here. There... back there."

"Don't panic. I know a short cut."

"Not this way, it's the wrong carriageway – that's a container lorry."

"I'll move over."

"Hell, it's gone through the central barrier and hit a coach. Where are you going now? That was a fence."

"'Salright. Tractors is the ultimate off-road ve-hic."

"Head for those lights. They might take us back on the road."

"No, Timbo – it's one of them stone thingies. There's weirdos in funny clothes..."

"They're standing in front of the stones. Turn, turn..."

"It don' wanna turn."

"Your sleeve's caught on that – look out."

"There's a lump of stone blocking this door, Timbo. What's it like your side? Timbo?"

Cathy Cade's Biography

Cathy is a former librarian whose retirement writing has, so far, been published in *Best of British* magazine, *Scribble* and – her proudest achievement – the *To Hull And Back Short Story Anthology 2018*. She can be found online at:

www.cathy-cade.com

13: FASHIONISTAS

by Peter J. Corbally

Inspired by: "Forget shrobing, it's all about JARVING" by Unity Blott, *Mail on Sunday*

Dropping her newspaper, Samantha gasped, "Oh my god, OMG." She had only just mastered shrobing and now it was passé. What to do? Where to turn for advice?

The phone was ringing for some seconds before Caitlin answered it.

"Have you seen the paper," gushed Samantha excitedly. "Shrobing is out, jarving is in."

"No, I don't believe it."

It was true and Samantha read the main points of the story to Caitlin.

Confusion reigned. They had committed themselves wholeheartedly to shrobing and had spent hundreds of pounds on it. To shrobe or not to shrobe hadn't been a question, it was de rigueur.

Sobbing, Caitlin ended the call.

A whole row of jackets would have to go. Tenderly stroking the sleeve of her favourite jacket, Samantha recalled the joys of shrobing. The walks in London's most exclusive streets simply to be seen shrobing. Meghan had confirmed it as the 'in' thing.

Then panic gripped her. She didn't own any jumpers. None that were new, anyway.

Her ringing phone brought her out of her reverie. Caitlin again. "What exactly is jarving?"

Peter J. Corbally's Biography

Retired teacher and small business owner. Now into amateur archaeology and trying flash fiction. A Yorkshireman exiled in Lancashire.

14: XARX'TH'S SEARCH FOR WORK

by Andrew Stiggers

Inspired by: "Migrant applies for 400 jobs before he finally got one" by Lincoln Tan, *NZ Herald*

Xarx'th wasn't sure about seeing the recruitment consultant but his partner had insisted.

"Your age is a problem." The human skims through Xarx'th's CV. "And the document is far too long."

"I see." He'd already laboured to condense a 120-year xeno-biology career into 10 pages.

"I suggest you adopt an Earth name, like Dave or Pedro. Xareth is—"

"*Xarx'th.*"

"Yes, Xarzeth is difficult to pronounce."

His family had been so excited in making the move from Talaxia. Studying Earth customs, taking language classes. But then Xarx'th struggled to find work and...

The recruiter studies his face. "Have you thought about wearing a hat?"

"A hat?"

"Yes. Something to cover that up." He points to the third eye on Xarx'th's forehead. "To be honest, employers will be intimidated by it. I would be. Although I'm used to your kind now."

The human is right — at his only job interview, the manager kept staring at it, and his blue skin of course. "OK."

"Great. I've got a good feeling about you, Xareth."

"*Xarx'th.*"

"You'll find work in no time."

Andrew Stiggers' Biography

Andrew Stiggers is a New Zealand writer. His work has appeared in *STORGY* among others, and his awards include winner of the 2017 Global Ebook Awards (Short Stories) and winner of the Trisha Ashley Award 2017 for best humorous story.

www.andrewstiggers.com

15: THE TYCOON

by Leslie Roberts

Inspired by: "Philip Green: 'There was banter but I meant no offence'" by Owen Bowcott, *The Guardian*

The tycoon leans into his sun lounger. "No interviews."

"It's not an interview." She hand-combs her fringe and sprawls into the adjacent lounger. "I want to apologise on behalf of the sisters."

He lifts his Ray-Bans, appraises her curves. "Sisters?" He replaces the shades. "Where's your mic?"

"I'm no journalist. It's awful, what they're doing to you. I can see it being banter. We do that all the time, where I work. 'Love' this, 'Darlin' that. A pat on the rump here and there. You tease someone for their accent, or their skin colour. What's the problem, if no hurt's intended?"

He sits up, studies her. "So what's your angle?"

She shrugs. "No angle. Just wanted to apologise."

"For the sisters?"

She nods. "I've always admired your charitable works."

"You seem like a nice girl. Fancy a drink?"

"Really? Wow. I mean... yeah. I wouldn't mind—"

"It's too public here. My room or yours?"

"Oh—"

"Mine's the Penthouse Suite. Coming?"

As he steers her to the foyer, a nearby sunbather trips the shutter and adjusts his directional microphone.

Leslie Roberts' Biography

Leslie Roberts lives in the south-west of England and has had modest competition successes. A collection of his stories – *Justice and other Short Stories* – has been published via Amazon's CreateSpace.

www.lesliemroberts.wordpress.com

16: LOVE AFTER BREXIT

by Alan Pattison

Inspired by: "Travel after Brexit: With only 200 days until UK leaves EU, here's what we do and don't know" by Simon Clader, *The Independent*

It all started on the Champs Élysées as they walked up towards the Arc de Triomphe. Claude turned towards her and said, "What is this that I have been hearing about the UK leaving the European Union and reduced opportunities for British people to live and work in other countries of the EU and vice versa?"

Margaret responded by saying, "I don't think that most of us know very much yet, but one thing I am sure of is that it will not split as I am still a German citizen and I have rights through my grandparents, as do you, to claim citizenship in Australia."

"So," said Claude, "we might have to change our plan to get married here in Paris, move to London."

"It may be possible," replied Margaret, "to take on the world from Sydney, if that's OK with you? They have a pretty opera house there which we could see on our honeymoon."

Alan Pattison's Biography

I am a semi-retired researcher of local history and author of fiction and poetry.

17: DON'T LET THE CAT OUT OF THE BAG

by John Holmes

Inspired by: "Sir Philip Green, other famous faces and why NDAs matter" by Rick Kelsey, *BBC*

Big trouble was certainly heading my way if Dad ever found out. Not that he even liked Smokey that much. But he sure wouldn't tolerate any cruelty towards her. And, to be honest, I didn't really feel I was being cruel, as I dangled her over the steamy bath. It was just funny. Feeling her wriggle gave me a kind of power.

Until she bit me.

And I dropped her.

A skinny streak of panicking cat scattering a wake of water, swooshing out through the door. The same door where my little sister was now standing. And where she was now screaming, "I'm telling Dad."

I grabbed her, put my hand over her mouth and forced her into my bedroom. I pushed her down onto the bed and held her until she calmed down. This one didn't bite.

Two weeks of my pocket money and the secret would be safe.

I made her cross her heart and hope to die.

Then she ran out of my room to look for Smokey.

Power restored.

I went for my bath.

VOLUME 1

John Holmes' Biography

Short story writer and cyclist. Published work in *The Guardian*, *Sunday Times*, *TES*. Co-author of *Rough Rides*. Former winner of *The Times* short story competition.

18: WHY DO MY NIPPLES HURT?

by Chris Espenshade

Inspired by: "Trump says synagogue should have had protection, calls for tougher death penalty laws" by Anonymous, *The Guardian*

"Really, mega-doses of estrogen? Will it work?"

"Well, we've tried everything else. Even when we carefully script a statement of compassion and empathy, he's unconvincing. He can't even act like he's a normal human. He blamed the victims; they should have had an armed guard. Who says that? He was more concerned with quashing calls for gun control than lamenting the real human grief being suffered in Pittsburgh, the Jewish community, the country."

"But estrogen? A sitting president?"

"Look, I reviewed the 24 times Obama had to tell the nation about a mass shooting. You could see the toll it was taking on the man; his empathy was palpable. Obama deeply grieved for the victims, the survivors, and the country. If we could get even a glimmer of that out of Trump, we might argue he just has trouble expressing those feelings. We've tried coaching and scripting, to no avail. We need a major change in his brain chemistry, and it will take quite a dose to offset his testosterone levels."

Chris Espenshade's Biography

An archaeologist, Chris Espenshade branched into creative writing in 2017. He's had flash fiction accepted by *Poached Hare, Fewer Than 500, Thrice Fiction, The Paragon Journal, Agora Journal, 81 Words*, and *The Dead Mule School of Southern Literature*.

19: AHEAD APART

by Francesca Pappadogiannis

Inspired by: "Royal SPLIT: Why Meghan is the reason for William and Harry's 'formal division'" by Paul Withers, *Express*

A source from Kensington Palace told the press about the conversation that had transpired in regards to the Royal split and why.

"The time has come for us to move from Nottingham Cottage as we need to make space for our first bundle of joy," said Meghan to Harry.

"I couldn't agree with you more, my love," replied Harry, in full agreement with his brother and best friend William, nodding their heads at the same time.

"We've reached a time in our lives when we no longer rely on each other, like we have in the past," exclaimed Harry formidably towards his brother.

"It may also help with the fact that our roles, needs and duties are changing and our families are both expanding," confirmed Kate.

"Not to mention that it will be a great deal easier to have two separate private offices managing our courts, specifically when I become the Prince of Wales with all its responsibilities, including the Duchy of Cornwall," explained William.

"Well then," said Meghan. "Let us toast to 'heads together, live apart'."

Francesca Pappadogiannis' Biography

A wife and mother to three awesome children. Freelance writer and poet. Profession: Dialectical Behavioural Therapist.

www.linkedin.com/in/francesca-pappadogiannis-1441ab14a

20: MAKING AMERICA GREAT

by Andrea Goyan

Inspired by: "72 hours in America: Three hate-filled crimes. Three hate-filled suspects" by Ray Sanchez and Melissa Gray, *CNN*

We haven't left our home in two weeks. Not since the first bombs took out the overpass. Not since graffiti covered the walls of the Piggly Wiggly a block from our house one day and bullets broke every pane of its glass the next. Not since places of worship were bathed in blood.

My cat purrs, oblivious. As a housecat, her life's always been restricted, so this isn't new to her, this life inside four walls.

We've covered our windows with plywood, the pre-cut sheets we store in our garage for hurricanes. We screwed them in place. My husband insisting, "A storm is coming, Tori, just another storm."

But it isn't the same. We're ill-prepared to ride out this plague of hatred.

We sit inside, while outside, predators lurk. Their brains on fire fueled by the rhetoric of our times, while our leaders do nothing but point the finger at each other

We sit inside.

I sip a cup of tea. Our milk has spoiled, so I drink it black. *A civil war is anything but civil*, I think.

Andrea Goyan's Biography

Andrea Goyan's short stories can be found in *Newfound Magazine*, and two anthologies, *Believe Me Not An Unreliable Anthology* and *It's About Time*. Over a dozen of her plays have been produced by theatres and festivals in Los Angeles.

@AndreaGoyan

21: BAH HUMBUG UPON AUSTERITY'S END

by Allen Ashley

Inspired by: "Budget 2018: Austerity finally coming to an end, says Hammond" by Anonymous, *BBC*

The era of Austerity is finally coming to an end. You may presume that it will be followed by an epoch of desperation, concurrent with a multiplication of spin. Scrounge the pavement for your pennies and spend them while you can before cash is taken out of circulation and we are all at the whim of universal credit card computer glitches that glitches that that reduce our spending power and earning capacity to less than zero.

Keep a little more of your income so we can grab it back on your booze and fags or ubiquitous VAT – a product of the European Union's precursor the Common Market, but bound to still be with us even if Brexit ever actually goes ahead.

Never publicly discuss religion and politics, we're told. Oh for God's sake… Happy days are here again, says our glorious Chancy Law. Again? Sorry, pal, when were they here before?

Allen Ashley's Biography

Allen Ashley is an award-winning writer and editor who has featured in all the Chris Fielden Challenges to date. His latest book is as co-editor (with Sarah Doyle) of *Humanagerie* (Eibonvale Press, UK) – animal-human liminality themed stories and poems. Allen works as a creative writing tutor.

www.allenashley.com

22: FOR WHOSE GOD AND WHICH COUNTRY?

by Kwame MA McPherson

Inspired by: "Pres. Trump abandons his umbrella on AF1" by Anonymous, *MSNBC on Facebook*

It was upturned, rolling to and fro on its axis. The breeze, light. A black metal pole rose up from within the middle, a leather-gripped handle at one end. The wide black umbrella was discarded on the brownstone's steps like his well-worn shoe, its blond-haired owner too busy to notice when he'd thrown it aside, before disappearing behind glass panelled doors.

Mark stood nearby under a dripping elm tree, trying to cover his head with a soggy broadsheet.

"Just like this darn country," he mumbled, watching the umbrella rock back and forth.

Glancing furtively along the avenue, he weighed his options. The road was clear, nothing moving but rain in grey sheets; just as the East Coast weatherman had predicted, remnants of some hurricane Mark couldn't name. Not that he cared; he was unemployed and wet, with holes in his shoes.

Shrugging, he headed across the street and, reaching the brownstone's steps, placed a foot on the lowest one. The wide door suddenly opened, the blond-haired man emerging. The man scanned him and smirked before grabbing up the umbrella.

Kwame MA McPherson's Biography

Kwame MA McPherson is an award-winning and prolific writer, poet, mentor and orator. As a storyteller, his prose reflects his life journey, travels and experiences. He is a contributor to various blogs, websites, anthologies and international magazines.

23: FRACT OR FICTION

by James Goodman

Inspired by: "Fracking halted at Lancashire site for third time after biggest earth tremor yet" by Josh Gabbatiss, *The Independent*

The car fell in.

Some sort of hole.

"Damn," he muttered.

His family sighed and shuffled. They peered anxiously at the suddenly unreliable ground.

"I told you..." trailed a tired voice. Nearby, a shale oil pump clacked.

They looked at the newly purchased house. Was it slumping? They looked at the bonnet of the car facing skywards. The indicators were flashing.

"The view's nice..." the tired voice tried again. The view looked as though an ocean liner had been half buried in it, all chimneys, lines and dials.

"Damn."

The air smelt damp, slightly inflammable. A child began sneezing and crying. His family stared at him, blank faced.

Headlines skittered through his mind: '"Earthquake rumours just scaremongering," says minister' – 'House prices hit new lows in area' – 'A RED event took place...'

A man in a hard hat and high-vis jacket was running towards them, shouting.

VOLUME 1

James Goodman's Biography

James Goodman is a secondary school teacher and amateur historian. He has been going on about the dangers of fracking for years.

24: THE PROMOTION OF LAWRENCE

by Mike Scott Thomson

Inspired by: "Justine Greening won't be Tory leader before Brexit. Afterwards, however..." by Martha Gill, *The Guardian*

With a deal dealt to deal with the deal not yet dealt but to be dealt with when the not-dealt deal be dealt with deftly, it was time for a change at the top.

This was a further headache The Board could do without. So they ratified a decision.

"No applications," they declared.

Those who had spent their career strenuously denying they wanted the job met this announcement with not a little consternation.

"What's all this surreptitious skulduggery?" said the Blonde Bombshell.

"Last year, you said you'd rather be bonked on the bonce by a breezeblock," said the Chairman. "No returns."

"Well, I said I did want it," piped up another.

"A most unfortunate breach in protocol. Those keenest for power are those least suited to it."

The Party was therefore stuck. To whom could they now turn?

A Machiavellian manipulator...

...authoritative yet disinterested...

...with a quantum-level understanding of simultaneous Leave AND Remain?

There could be only one.

The Chairman bent down and nuzzled the new leader's collar.

"Meow," said the now ex-Chief Mouser to the Treasury.

Mike Scott Thomson's Biography

Mike Scott Thomson's short stories have been published by journals and anthologies, and have won the occasional award, including first prize in Chris Fielden's inaugural To Hull And Back competition. Based in south London, he works in broadcasting.

www.mikescottthomson.com

25: HARRY

by Michael Rumsey

Inspired by: "Real Madrid sack Julen Lopetegui as manager" by Anonymous, *BBC Sport*

Harry read the article and shrugged. People in other jobs get sacked too and now it was his turn. These days they called it redundancy. Same thing really...

There'd been rumours for weeks. Then, yesterday, at The Grange Nursing Home, Fred the storekeeper said Matron had a letter, no more deliveries from Princess Street. Grace, the secretary at Head Office, had hinted at sweeping changes. Yeah right, new broom, in with the new and all that.

Now, young Robert had invited him to the office, to tell him face to face, and so he should. 40 years, man and boy, by dear old Sam Maitland's side from the corner shop, right up the ladder to Princess Street Supermarket, until Sam's death six months ago.

"Deliveries from 1st Jan next year," Robert began, "will all be made from our new warehouse on Greenways Industrial Estate. Not just groceries, but a whole host of new products. I know Dad would agree, it's imperative we give first class service. Harry, that's why I'm asking you to manage the whole thing."

Michael Rumsey's Biography

Michael has contributed to all our challenges. As a keen administrator of our Authors of the Flash Fiction Writing Challenges page on Facebook he says, to use his own words, "He sees it as a way to stay in the news."
www.facebook.com/mrumsey

26: YOU'RE FIRED

by Dr Betty

Inspired by: "Missile threat alert for Hawaii a false alarm; officials blame employee who pushed 'wrong button'" by Zachary Cohen, *CNN*

Time to make America great again.

Five minutes to impact, Mr President.

It was only Hawaii, after all. The loss would be tragic, but also acceptable compared to those Commie asses being blown sky high.

Four minutes to impact, Mr President.

Codes were entered. Protocols by-passed. A decisive president is a strong president.

Three minutes, Mr President.

Today, he would trump himself. Today, he would trump the world and show them all what they were dealing with.

Two minutes, Mr President.

The hand of POTUS hovered over the button, not in thought but for effect.

One minute.

The President chuckled. He pressed down. Hard. Ratings and missiles soared.

Mr President, fake news.

Someone had pressed the wrong button.

Russian retaliation was brutal. America was *fired*.

VOLUME 1

Dr Betty's Biography

Dr Betty is a parent, teacher and humanitarian. She observes with a keen eye for the absurd, seeking common ground in differing perspectives – a challenge too great when writing about Trump.

27: LEST WE FORGET

by Geja Hadderingh

Inspired by: "Family's long wait for pupil killed in crash" by Anonymous, *IOL*

It is clear that your mother has been back again with another bunch of cheap flowers and her roll of Sellotape. It is not the original lamp post. The council had quickly removed the remnants of that one. The replacement one is now mummified by your mother's tape. Scarves and shirts have long gone. As have your fans. Blown away in the wind of time.

But your mum hasn't forgotten.

Neither have I.

You, the famous footballer, who had often played at Wembley.

Me, a runner, who enjoyed the solitude of running alone.

For weeks after the crash, the newspapers were full of your story.

I received a brief mention in the local press: 'An unlucky jogger, in the wrong place at the wrong time.'

Your death seemed to allow forgiveness to the fact that you were a drunk driver.

Your fame softened your supporters' minds.

I work my mouth and spit violently at the flowers.

"Lest We Forget," I say out loud, and turn my Scoot-Mobile round and head back to my one bedroomed flat.

Geja Hadderingh's Biography

A Dutch citizen dipping her toe into the water of short story writing for the first time.

28: BLUE TEARS

by Lynne Chitty

Inspired by: "Leicester City owner 'on board crashed helicopter'" by Anonymous, *BBC*

My scarf looked tatty amongst the rest, but I didn't care. It was my bestest thing in the whole world and as I carefully laid it down, I was proud. Proud to have known him. Proud to have shaken his hand. "Well done, son," he'd said when I'd come off the pitch and my heart had grown that big I thought it would explode. I didn't wash for a whole week, not 'til me mum had said I really did need to shower as I was beginning to stink a bit.

I'd been one of the mascots, you see. I'd carried the ball right out to the middle. Had my photo taken with the captains and then sprinted off to watch from the side. That's when he'd seen me.

So I gave him my scarf. The one my dad gave me before he got cancer. Going to games was our special time and when we won the league, we cried and laughed and sang that many songs...

R.I.P. Mr Vichai.

You were the best.

Just like my dad.

Lynne Chitty's Biography

I live in Devon and write mainly reflections. I have a short story in Ann Cleeves' *Offshore* and have published a novel *Out of the Mist*. I'm a Deacon, a spurs fan and training for the London Marathon.

29: BREAKING THE RULES

by John Notley

Inspired by: "Freemasons throw open lodge doors – and answer questions on secrecy, corruption concerns and rolling up trouser legs" by Mike Laycock, *The York Press*

I was interested to read that the local Masonic Lodge was to open its doors to the public one evening. My dad, dead a couple of years, had been a freemason and instilled in me the strict moral code that members were obliged to follow.

"Son," he said, "it's not about what you get out, but what you put in that counts." I had always thought it was a cosy club for making business contacts, but that's not how he saw it. I had now turned 18 and felt it would be a good time to find out more.

I arrived on the day and was shown around by a mentor who was happy to answer my questions. He dispelled many myths about secret societies, satanic rituals and world domination which abound. Even that rolling up their trouser legs had a reason.

When I later went to my membership interview, I was disappointed that they refused to admit me. "Sorry, sir, we can't let you in dressed like that."

"I thought wearing shorts would save time," I apologised.

John Notley's Biography

John, a retired travel agent, has written a number of stories over the years but has yet to receive the fame and adulation he feels due to him. Perhaps he will receive his reward in another place.

30: IN STITCHES

by E. F. S. Byrne

Inspired by: "Surgery students 'losing dexterity to stitch patients'" by Sean Coughlan, *BBC*

"Get the sewing machine, love."

"You can't be serious. You know you can't believe everything you read."

"Get the sewing machine. When Johnny comes home, I want to make sure he is patched up properly."

"He'll be fine. It was you who lost a leg."

"Didn't lose it. Had it blown from under me."

"You always had big feet."

"If he has anything missing, anything cut up, I want you to sew it back." Jake looked admiringly at the curtain hemline, the hole in his shirt finely knitted back, unlike his missing leg.

"Jake, you need to calm down."

"I'm not having my son mutilated by a so-called doctor raised on the internet. All day playing with screens, can't sew a button on, never cut and stitch a war wound. Those stupid computer games. Nobody knows how to win a real war anymore. Or tidy up afterwards."

Mary got out the sewing machine just to keep him quiet. She hoped their son would be alright. She couldn't face another argument over how to put him back together.

E. F. S. Byrne's Biography

E. F. S. Byrne works in education. With two teenage children, he has finally found more time to devote to his writing. He is working on a range of material from short flash to full-length novels.

www.efsbyrne.wordpress.com

31: IS ANYONE THERE?

by Tony Thatcher

Inspired by: "Daily Mail Showbiz Pages" by Various, *Daily Mail*

"That was 'Tequila Sunrise' on So Easy FM. And the first person to ring and tell me the name of the band will win this fabulous bird feeder."

Two records later he made a phone call.

"I know it's late, but I need a favour."

"It's three in the morning. What do you want?"

"Could you ring and tell me the name of the band is the Eagles?"

"What?"

"I've had no replies to a question I asked. It's making it look like I have no listeners."

"That's possibly because you don't. And if no one is listening, why does it matter? Goodbye."

The DJ cursed the disconnected phone and threw it at the glass walls of his semi-dark cell. Fading out the music, he resumed the cosy manner he liked to think he was famous for.

"I'm afraid we've got a few technical problems so I'm going to have to put that competition on hold. I do apologise to all of you who've been trying to get through."

Tony Thatcher's Biography

Most of my life has been spent designing stuff. When I'm not doing that I write short stories and flash fiction. One day I will finish my best selling award winning soon to be a major movie novel project.

32: SOAKED PANTS ARE THE LEAST OF OUR ISSUES

by Louise Burgess

Inspired by: "Venice under water as deadly storms hit Italy" by Anonymous, *BBC*

It finally hit the news. 'Venice under water'. It was shown with pictures of smiling 'locals' splashing about in the streets as if it was a lovely new addition to the city. It almost seemed like it was planned to get new tourists to visit Venice with officials even claiming that almost 75% of it was now submerged, meaning it was almost the next Atlantis.

It wasn't like that for me though, as I waded through murky water to what was once my bookshop. Stepping through the shattered front window as the door no longer worked, I searched for any remains of what once was my pleasured livelihood, climbing onto the 6ft high bookcases. I had to salvage as many of the leftover books as I could. I still needed to make money to feed my daughter and survive until the insurance paid out.

Grabbing the precious books into my backpack, holding it up above my head as I slipped back into the dirty water ignoring the wetness of my soaked pants, I lumbered my way home.

Louise Burgess' Biography

Louise Burgess is a writer for pleasure and competitions around her hectic family life. If you would like to read other short stories by Louise, please visit:
www.loopybwritingpage.wordpress.com

33: BROWN OF THE CED

by Steven Barrett

Inspired by: "Police 'save the day' after bringing riot van to six-year-old's party" by Anonymous, *BBC*

Detective Sergeant Brown faced his team in the briefing room.

"What's it this time, sir?" asked Constable Arnolds.

"Dinosaurs."

A murmur went around the room.

"And we've only got 20 minutes."

Could they pull it off? Brown wondered. It would be their toughest challenge yet. But that's why this team had been put together. The CED — Children's Entertainment Division — had been formed to step in if a kid's party found itself without entertainment. Already, they'd been penguin jugglers (not easy with flippers), fairy-tale princesses and clowns. That time, they'd even arranged for the van to fall apart.

He showed them the whiteboard displaying a diagram of the house and the van's route.

"Arnolds, you're a Stegosaurus. Aziz, Triceratops. Jenkins, it's the Diplodocus for you."

"Can't I be a Velociraptor, sir? They're way cooler."

In the van, Brown looked at his team through the jaws of his Tyrannosaurus Rex outfit. The team were practising their roaring. *Such attention to detail*, he thought. As they started rehearsing the 'Hokey Cokey', it made him proud to think of how far they'd come.

Steven Barrett's Biography

Steven was born and lives in Edinburgh. He tries keeping fit by running and enjoys entering races. He has just started writing short stories, after years of just thinking about doing it.

34: STRUT, TURN, SNAP

by Clare Tivey

Inspired by: "Stray kitty rightfully reclaims fashion show catwalk" by Rachelle Bergstein, *New York Post*

Not to be ungrateful, Yasmin was glad of the work. It's not easy for an aging woman in this profession, but A TIGER? No mention of the cat from the booking agent... must get a new booking agent.

Runway shows had become outlandish and demands on models increasingly unreasonable. The Tiger was supposedly tame, but the way she yanked the heavy chain-lead made Yasmin nervous. The two beauties scrutinised each other. Those yellow eyes... was she to be supper? Not that she would make a satisfying meal; she hadn't eaten carbs since 1992.

The outfit consisted of barely there chainmail, and 7-inch heels, a half size too small. Her feet would avenge later, in the form of blisters. The lights were hot, the music loud and angry. Her feet burned and the tiger, all 140kg of her, was not happy.

Then, as quick as a camera flash: the hunger, the harassment, the humiliating outfits, the fake air kisses... As she reached the end of the runway, Yasmin turned, let go of the tiger's lead and let the cat walk.

Clare Tivey's Biography

I live in Suffolk with my partner, Matt, enjoying the countryside, cycling and wild swimming. I write short stories for fun and catharsis. My ambition is to have a whole book published one day.

35: PEA-BRAIN

by W R Daniel

Inspired by: "Removing items in ears and noses 'costs NHS £3m a year'" by Anonymous, *BBC*

The doctor's face was magnified through the convex glass as the boy felt the cold, rounded tips grasp the blockage. The doctor slowly retracted his hand, successfully extricating the garden pea from the boy's nostril.

"All done?" asked the boy's mother. She was beginning to grow impatient after having to rush to A&E during *Strictly*.

The doctor washed his hands in the stainless steel basin.

"This young man has been very lucky. Peas inserted into the nasal passage can work their way upwards into the cerebral cortex, where they begin to break down, surrounding the brain in a green mush. This 'mush' slowly expands, shrinking the brain until the patient develops what we call 'Pea-Brain'."

"Goodness. Is there a cure?" asked the boy's mother.

"More peas, Mrs Jenkins," said the doctor, drying his hands with a paper towel. "Lots of them. And other veg too. Eaten correctly they should boost the immune system enough to avoid any ill-effects."

The boy gulped. He certainly wasn't going to tell them about the piece of carrot lodged in his ear.

W R Daniel's Biography

W R Daniel was born in Manchester in the early 1980s. He writes short fiction, watches far too many 1970s B-movie horror films and collects vintage science fiction novels.

www.wrdanielauthor.com

36: BULLYBOYS AND BILLIONAIRES

by Edmund Piper

Inspired by: "Lord Hain was right to use of Parliamentary privilege – our laws are failing modern society" by Rupa Huq, *The Telegraph*

Blow a whistle, take on the establishment, uncover a can of worms, and you're in big trouble – disturbing the cosy is a mortal sin. Might as well give up. Go with the tide, keep your head down, turn a blind eye, mind nobody else's business, drag out the under-carpet sweeper and you're in with a chance.

Catch a tycoon in a naughty and you can make a packet in non-disclosure. He thinks he can get away with absolutely anything and he can, so long as his purse is big enough, or some fair-minded busybody in the privilege safe-house doesn't spill the beans.

Take a national treasure down a peg or two with a wild accusation – true or not, there's no smoke, they will say. Who then is kosher? If he's rich, could be the piper is being paid to play his tune. The rest of us aren't flush enough to buy our good character. But who said bullyboy threats and intimidation are not just as effective?

Edmund Piper's Biography

Born in rural Sussex, Cambridge law degree, thence to a lifetime of wedded bliss, publishing and IT. Now free to enjoy life, exempted from working for my salary and excused household chores.

37: GETTING THE HUMP

by David Silver

Inspired by: "Heatwaves are lasting twice as long as 50 years ago, sub-zero days are disappearing and tropical nights are occurring in Middlesbrough, Met Office climate change study finds" by Danyal Hussain, *Mail Online*

Colin peered out from the camel transporter vehicle and, with front feet splayed, carefully descended the ramp. "Where are we?" he asked grumpily. And then he spat out.

Crispin, the other camel, followed his companion down onto the beach and remarked, "I don't think much of this sand. I reckon it's that ersatz stuff, not like the real thing back in Africa."

Colin spat again. "I'm just relieved to be off that plane."

"Actually," said Crispin, "I sneaked a look at the flight manifest before we set off. We're now in a place called Uk."

"Uk?" queried Colin. "What sort of a name is Uk? Sounds Biblical to me." Colin sniffed the air. "Hang on a second. I detect the presence of fish and chips. I reckon this must be the UK, the new hotspot for exotic holidays."

"Oh, no," Crispin responded. "We must be here because it's too sweltering for the donkeys. The human kiddies will ride on us instead."

And although Crispin was a lot posher than Colin, he spat out, too.

VOLUME 1

David Silver's Biography

David Silver was a reporter, sub-editor and columnist on various newspapers in Greater Manchester, England. He retired in 2002 and from 2011-2016 wrote a column for *The Courier*, a weekly newspaper for UK expatriates in Spain.

38: WHAT DO WE TELL THE CHILDREN?

by D.G. Kaye

Inspired by: "The Children at the Trump Rallies" by Damon Winter, *New York Times*

"Quick, Dave, switch the channel," Molly shouted to her husband as they both scrambled for the remote control.

The president appeared on TV once again, spewing his bombastic vitriol against the innocent victims fleeing their countries in desperation for a better life.

Little Billy slid in with his slippery socks and a disheartening stare. Only five years old, yet, his mind a giant sponge filled with curiosity and a heart just as big, abundant with compassion.

"Dave, how long can we keep our son hidden from this prejudice?"

"Mamma, I feel sad," Billy lamented. "I don't know why the bigger kids at school are picking on my friends. What did they do? They're too scared to play with me at school in the playground."

"I knew this day would come, Dave." Molly's heart sank in despair.

Dave lifted his son onto his lap. "Billy, sometimes other kids forget to be kind. Remember, kindness is in everybody's hearts. Why don't we call your friend Abduhl to come play? We'll show him our kindness by giving him a hug."

Temporary damage control.

VOLUME 1

D.G. Kaye's Biography

Canadian author D.G. Kaye is a nonfiction/memoir writer who shares her stories about life experiences, matters of the heart and women's issues, hoping to inspire and empower others. Find her books on Amazon.
   www.dgkayewriter.com

39: THE LOSS OF A CUNNING LINGUIST

by Guy Monson

Inspired by: "Top linguist: 'I'm leaving the UK because of the disaster of Brexit'" by Nosheen Iqbal, *Observer Magazine*

Commander Hardcastle sprang to his feet and stopped his alarm 0.6 seconds before it went off.

04:55 GMT.

He strode to the shower, washed in the icy torrent, exited the cubicle, rolled across the rug to dry himself and put on his uniform.

04:58 GMT. SMS: *Code Red. Car outside.*

Blue lights illuminated the stairs; he descended three at a time.

"Sir." The officer opened the door, two others trained weapons on the street.

"SITREP?"

"It's red, sir. Briefing on arrival. PM insisted on you."

Richard entered Cabinet Office Briefing Room-A, took in a sombre picture of Churchill visiting a bombed-out Coventry, then saw the even more sombre face of the Prime Minister.

"Richard, we thought Brexit couldn't get worse. It just did."

"Ma'am?"

The PM pushed *The Observer* across the capacious walnut table and he instantly took in the headline: 'Alex Rawlings, named the country's most multilingual student in 2012, is moving to Barcelona next month.'

"Oh, cruel world... cometh the hour, deserteth the 'teacher and app developer'," sobbed the PM.

Richard saw the revolver... 0.6 seconds too late.

Guy Monson's Biography

Guy Monson worked as a radio journalist before going into business. Despite having a degree in Psychology, Guy's positive view of his fellowman has proved to be both robust and enduring and he's at his happiest playing devil's advocate.

40: THE CHESS PLAYER

by Klaus Gehling

Inspired by: "Unaccompanied Minors in Germany" by Anonymous, *Federal Office for Migration and Refugees*

They were sitting in a railway station.

"Blitz, how much?" mumbled the boy.

"Ten, if you win," his opponent sneered.

The boy gnashed his teeth and made the first move. His game started in Iraq. After being robbed, he won his first game against a captain of a ship sailing to Greece.

A Greek conductor looked away, after losing his match, when the young, hungry boy, together with others, clung to an air compressor beneath the train. Some lost their grip.

His chess skills saved him from starving in a Baltic jail.

He stared at his chess board and his thoughts wandered to his father who had taught him the game. Where was he? Was he still alive?

His opponent coughed, tapped on the table and said, "Your move."

He won his game.

Klaus Gehling's Biography

Klaus is a retired psychologist and psychotherapist living in Germany. He spends his time writing stories, traveling, playing chess and his guitar. He loves writing 'odd stories', which are often inspired by his professional experience.

41: THE PITS

by Teresia Nicolas

Inspired by: "The absolute pits: how underarms became the new frontier of advertising" by Anonymous, *The Guardian*

It started with Dove pomegranate.

The audition was tough. So many applicants. Such few positions.

"You can do this," my boyfriend kept saying, massaging my tense shoulders, making murmuring sounds of generic encouragement. My heart was beating erratically.

Finally, it was my turn. I went into a small cubicle. Two men sat behind a white desk, faces bland, serious. They looked on as I removed my jacket and raised my arm in the air. High in the air. Like a victory gesture. I had shaved the night before — would it be enough?

"What is your commute?" asked the man to the left. His piercing gaze made me squirm.

"Piccadilly line," I squeaked, slightly horse from the adrenaline. My arm was still reaching for the sky. I could smell my own musk. "Hammersmith to Finsbury Park."

The man nodded. They exchanged a glance. My heart leapt.

"The fragrance will be pomegranate," said the second man, in hushed tones. "Can you cope with that?"

I lowered my arm at last, slowly, hot triumph rushing through my veins.

"It's my favourite."

Teresia Nicolas' Biography

I'm an English teacher of the International Baccalaureate, living in Sweden. This is the type of stuff I like to do with my students. I had lots of fun.

42: THE REVOLUTIONARY WORM

by Jon Drake

Inspired by: "Human chain finds a novel way to move independent bookshop" by Charlie Parker, *The Times*

You may think me a Lumbricus terrestris by my number or shape, but I am no simple earthworm. I am a Hellus librorum, or a bookworm to you and me. I extend by over 250 segments, hermaphroditic by nature yet subtly coordinated in linear form to achieve my movement.

I was born in October and of revolution. I seek no profit for my radical passion or disruption from my co-operative beliefs, but I long for community where once there was capitalism.

I move away from excessive financial demand to voluntary public patronage, reaching the hearts of those needing my existence and endeavour. For a brief moment I am inherently 'book-bosomed', powered by 'bibliosmiacs' and at temporary risk of becoming 'the bibliobibuli'.

Yet I survive by the bibliophilic nature of my parts – independent in spirit, free in enterprise and emotional in existence. I am deeply and successfully moved by it all.

Jon Drake's Biography

Jon Drake is a retired secondary head teacher who, as a trained scientist and educationalist, wants to explore the more creative sides of life in retirement. He lives in the Cotswolds using the surroundings as inspiration for writing and music-making.

43: PUT HIM DOWN

by Dora Bona

Inspired by: "Savage reaction to horse being euthanised after Melbourne Cup 'tragedy'" by Matt Toogood, *news.com.au*

If I'd known I would end up here, I would most certainly have thrown a race years ago. This is delightful.

No more gruelling training sessions and being dragged from a nice warm stable in the early morning frost. No more strict diets with unpalatable, bland food. No more listening to the snorting and stomping from those jealous stable nags with no breeding, who couldn't win a three-legged mule race. I can eat as much luscious green grass as I like, sleep 'til noon if it pleases me, and watch as much TV as I want.

Those humans are incredible beasts, aren't they? Probably the finest specimens on two legs. I'm not sure if they should be bred for such barbaric sports as racing though. Did you catch the sensational finish of the 100 metre hurdles? That Cliff Moher, poor thing... he fractured his shoulder after a fall at the last hurdle and had to be euthanised.

Headlines are all over the news. Calls for the nation to stop the sport that stops a nation. Hmm... overkill, don't you think?

Dora Bona's Biography

A freelance writer from Oswestry, Shropshire, who loves good stories – reading them, writing them and capturing them with a camera.

44: WOLVES

by Pete Armstrong

Inspired by: "Zoo finishes with Wolves" by Anonymous, *8 Sidor*

And so the wolves are gone. Vanished. Cut down in their prime. Well, perhaps just a little past their prime, but they must still be annoyed about it. Civilisation removes another inconvenient touch of nature, and we can all choose from a variety of lupine screensavers to remember them by.

Our great home continues to rotate forward through the Cosmos and, to the un-detecting eye, not much will have changed. Ancient trees remain unmolested in Kolmården forest. Squirrels and rabbits, lesser beasts, play in safety, running unchallenged down the tracks and runs that have been laid out by generations.

But in the shadows behind the trees, no more will savage hunters glide silently past. No longer will they glare unseen through the leaves, malevolent in their ravenous fury. The wooden trunks will never again echo with the empty timbre of their noiselessly padding feet.

We shall meet no more on this green and brown, earthen land.

But when we do come face to face again, in the leafy skog of Valhalla's wooded gardens, then surely they will *HOWL*.

Pete Armstrong's Biography

Pete lives in a leafy suburb in central Sweden. He mostly looks after children, and he writes stuff and listens to Bach when they are not about. He remains unsure about how he landed such a cushy number.

www.armstrong99.com

45: HOPE

by Sam Nichols

Inspired by: "Plastic-eating caterpillar could munch waste, scientists say" by Helen Briggs, *BBC*

We thought we'd cracked it. Plastic waste was turning our home into an abomination of our own creation. No one cared enough, and those that did had lost hope we could turn things around. Without hope, everything was lost. Plastic had entered the food and water cycles, millions died daily.

But then, a very special caterpillar that had by some miracle evolved to consume and breakdown plastic was discovered. A gift from Mother Earth. After giving up on waiting for us to turn things around, she had taken matters into her own hands. We still had a lot of work to do, to put these caterpillars into mass production, but slowly, results came in. And then sped up.

Was this a cruel, ironic joke on mankind? Or another gift, sending us back to simpler times?

The caterpillars did not stop at plastic waste. They evolved and began to eat up all of our plastic world. At least it stopped us fighting.

Once there's no more plastic and the caterpillars die out, hopefully we can start again.

Sam Nichols' Biography

Working as an offshore geologist, Sam has plenty of time to focus on his writing during his time off at home. Focused on fictional short stories, he hopes to work on an extended story in the near future.

46: NO FURTHER ACTION

by John Gisby

Inspired by: "There are billions of Earth like worlds in the Universe and we are not alone. There are billions of Earth like worlds in the Universe and we are alone. One of those statements is true." by Professor Brian Cox, *Human Universe*

A report for the meeting of the next Galaxy Senate was a critical review of an item in its space exploration programme.

Introducing this, the titan senator reported that the last five surveys had confirmed that planet Earth continued to have great diversity of tribes, religions and political beliefs. These created large blocs of entrenched social instability, wide spread malnutrition and forced migration. He said the planet had a long record of wars and rebellions. International cooperation was limited to activity by charities. Corruption in governments, their bureaucracies, and in business was widespread.

In response to a question, he gave his opinion that the continuation of life on Earth was becoming uncertain. Species had become extinct, proven resources were limited and inevitable climate changes were largely ignored.

In debate, members expressed only disadvantages in associating with planet Earth.

The chair proposed that further surveys of planet Earth should not be undertaken for five years and its attempts to establish contacts with other planets should continue to be ignored.

Both proposals were passed unanimously.

VOLUME 1

John Gisby's Biography

A former army officer, made an invention then developed a medical charity. After a second retirement took up writing and has items published in *The Political Quarterly*, *Church Times*, *British Army Journal* and *Scribble*.

47: A LESSON LEARNED

by Jack Caldwell-Nichols

Inspired by: "Boozy feral pig steals beer, gets drunk and starts fight with a cow" by Rob Williams, *The Independent*

It was just another typical evening, under the shimmering stars, combining to make up the long, mystical flow of lights, in what the human tongue names the Milky Way.

The herd was mingled together, with Buffalo Bill again in a mood, not wanting to socialise. Daisy, Angus and Shelly knew that Bill didn't like to be called Buffalo. The rest of us were happily grazing when a smelly, filthy, drunken hog somehow had the sheer audacity to come barnstorming into our field.

"Oi," he oinked at us, fully taking advantage of his surprise tactics. "You lot are a bunch of smelly old, goody four hoofed plonkers, you know that?"

Angus, known for his hot hoofiness, decided to take the bull by the horns.

"You're not welcome here anymore, Kevin. I've had just about enough of your horsin' around. Now go home, you're drunk," he mooed.

And with that, the herd carried on grazing.

Kevin was shocked. It really hit home how badly he had treated his fellow animals and vowed to be sober from that day forth.

Jack Caldwell-Nichols' Biography

Amateur author and budding bowler, with a penchant for posters and tendencies to tiptoe across long, lethal lengths whilst balancing a balloon on my thigh. My name is Jack.

48: THOUGHTS AND PRAYERS

by David Rosenblum

Inspired by: "California bar shooting: Victim's mother says she doesn't want prayers, she wants 'no more guns'" by Rebecca Joseph, *Global News*

I saw her sad, watery eyes. She was a mother of a person who survived one mass murder but didn't survive the latest one. She angrily denounced 'thoughts and prayers', wanting gun control.

Her son was one of twelve that didn't survive.

It was the second time in three weeks I couldn't sleep, except fitfully.

The previous murderous serial slaughter of innocents really hit home.

This was my synagogue. My place of worship. My sanctuary.

Not really. But it was similar to mine. Two of the synagogue victims were brothers who greeted new patrons at Pittsburgh synagogue, with friendly faces and warm handshakes.

I felt the bitterness and anger and hatred that the California mum felt, even though I did not lose anyone personally. But I did in my heart.

'Thoughts and prayers' is not the answer. Gun control and improved mental health screenings and elimination of weapons of death and multi-shot magazines is.

I don't want to hear 'thoughts and prayers' again. Just the sound of love and laughter and kindness, and the elimination of hatred.

David Rosenblum's Biography

I have been writing short stories and memoirs for years. Nothing published. I have been a health care administrator, physician and professor for most of my adulthood. Have three grown children I am very proud of. Trying to embark on this new career. Second life, sort of.

49: LIVING IN THE PAST

by Malcolm Richardson

Inspired by: "Thousands stay tuned to black and white TV" by Jack Malvern, *The Times*

Geoff settled down in his favourite armchair, a can of Double Diamond poised on the nest of tables. Myra switched on the television and waited for it to warm up. They loved their 12-inch black and white set. Geoff bought it at a car boot sale in 1997 for a fiver, complete with a free copy of that week's *Radio Times*. It fitted snugly into their compact lounge in their two up, two down 1930s terraced house. They loved their home; it was like living in Coronation Street.

When the analogue signal was terminated, Geoff bought one of those digital set top box thingamabobs. It enabled them to watch weekly repeats of *Dixon of Dock Green* on a Saturday night and the occasional Agatha Christie play on a Sunday afternoon.

Neither of them could cope with these newfangled hi-fi Bluetooth gadgets. Downloading songs just didn't make sense. Their 1950s Philips Radiogram, complete with original valves, still worked perfectly. Geoff loved listening to the home service and Myra treasured her collection of Elvis Presley 78s.

Malcolm Richardson's Biography

Malcolm started out writing about cycling for magazines. Later, he progressed to writing fiction. Last year he discovered flash fiction. This year he won a flash competition, has been runner-up in another and had two flashes published in charity anthologies.

50: I WAS ONLY FOLLOWING ORDERS

by Allan Tweddle

Inspired by: "Soldiers in north Yorkshire warned not to eat Greggs in uniform as it 'makes them look unprofessional'" by James Morris, *Evening Standard*

We gasped as the captain posted the order. We'd heard rumours, but they'd seemed too incredible.

"Under no circumstances should troops stand outside Greggs eating pasties while in uniform."

"What about my human rights?" Slasher said.

"The general says it's bringing the regiment into disrepute. He doesn't want the civvies thinking we're lazy fat slobs," Smithy said.

"There's only one thing to do," I said.

"It's a sacrifice, but you're right," Jock agreed.

We hit Greggs at 13.00 hours.

"Six cheese pasties and six steak bakes, please love," I said.

Mouth open and eyes wide, she shook out a paper bag and shovelled the delicious golden slabs inside.

"What the hell's this?" the captain shouted, his bulk filling the doorway.

"Just following orders, sir," I said.

He stared at our naked six-packs, bulging quads and pulsing biceps, then his eyes swept across the full counter. He thrust his menacing face to within inches of mine. Then he reached up and began to unbutton his jacket.

"Make mine a steak bake," he ordered.

I saluted. What else could I do?

VOLUME 1

Allan Tweddle's Biography

Allan lives in London with his wife, kids and Labrador, Yoda. His ambition is to write the next *Da Vinci Code* then retire to the sun on the proceeds. It's not going well so far.

51: WHO WERE YOU?

by Betty Hattersley

Inspired by: "A Mandarin Duck Mysteriously Appears in Central Park, to Birders' Delight" by Julia Jacobs, *New York Times*

Bill always wanted to be in the army. Although it was a time of war, against their parents' wishes, he and his pals joined various army regiments.

Bill's regiment was posted to Tel Aviv. Immediately after arriving, whilst away from the barracks, he had a strange feeling, as if he'd been there before.

Returning back to his barracks, he was approached by his comrades. "Someone's been looking for you."

"What's his name?" Bill asked. "What did he look like?"

"Can't really describe him. He wouldn't give his name and we weren't sure what uniform he wore," they replied. "He said he knew your family and wished you all the best for the future."

Once they were all demobbed, Bill asked everyone if they knew who visited the barracks that day during the war. No one knew. In fact, they'd all been posted in other countries.

That unsolved mystery stayed with him for nearly 70 years. But, after he was told of the visit, he knew he would return home safe and sound.

VOLUME 1

Betty Hattersley's Biography

I have had many short stories and poems published in magazines, newspapers, greeting cards etc.

52: A SHORT-LIVED SPELL OF HAPPINESS

by Lesley Anne Truchet

Inspired by: "'Back from the dead': Aigali Supygaliev turns up two months after burial in Kazakhstan" by Anonymous, *Sky News*

"I'd love a face and figure like yours." The hairdresser didn't know how much her words meant to me. Brand-new expensive clothing, styled hair, makeup and a manicure. What a transformation.

I made coffee, another new pleasure, and gazed around my recently installed bespoke kitchen.

The plane crash had killed all onboard, including my husband. I went through the necessary public display of grief. God help me, I was delighted to be rid of him.

I'd found thousands of banknotes in his study, previously locked against my intrusion. To think he'd made me wear thin rags and go barefoot indoors, without heating. We'd lived on cheap unappetising food and drank water.

The front door banged. Familiar footsteps. Dizzy with shock, my mouth dry, I fought to speak coherently. "I... I thought you were on the fatal flight to Dubai."

He took a step towards me, his face menacing. "You've been spending my money. Lots of it." His hands reached out. He had come back from death. I was probably going to mine.

VOLUME 1

Lesley Anne Truchet's Biography

Lesley Truchet has been writing for several years and has a number of short stories, articles and poems published on paper and on the internet. She is currently writing her first novel.

53: THE WOMAN IN THE BOOKSHOP

by Stacey George

Inspired by: "Waterstones snaps up Foyles to open new chapter in fight against Amazon" by Deirdre Hipwell, *The Times*

"I wonder if that lady will be in today."

"Yes, we haven't seen her for a while."

A lady came into the bookshop around the same time every afternoon. She always looked sad and she seemed to be gazing up the flight of stairs that lead onto the floor where the cafe was situated. Occasionally she would go and take a seat, usually at the same table. Tears would be in her eyes and she would seem to be looking at someone in the opposite seat, only there was nobody sitting there. She hadn't been seen for months.

A customer, overhearing this conversation, said, "Excuse me, I was that woman's neighbour. She passed away some months ago. She sometimes used to meet her friend in your cafe. He died too and, on top of the death of her mother, it was too much for her to bear. I think she died of a broken heart. That's just my opinion and we should never judge a book by its cover."

The whole shop fell silent.

Stacey George's Biography

I have written three books and all the proceeds from their sales go to help the homeless, who sleep on our streets each night, as well as knitting scarves which I give to the nuns to help in their work.

54: DONALD EXPOSES FAKE NEWS

by Vaki Kokkinaki

Inspired by: "Russian national charged with attempting to interfere in 2018 midterms" by Katelyn Polantz, *CNN*

Frankly, I've had enough of those tales about Russians meddling in US politics. Can't you see that the US President was created by Gyro Gearloose in the image of my obnoxious cousin Gastone, who's behind the whole thing and even lent his hairstylist to the cause?

Don't let his charming ways fool you, for Gastone is more vulture than duck. He had the android named after me, because he liked the idea of the press dragging my name through the gutter. He also convinced Scrooge to fund his sick project, under the pretext that something should be done about the Disney Princesses who stole Duckburg's glory and posed a threat to his wealth. My uncle is still waiting for Elsa and Anna of Arendelle to get deported as illegal immigrants.

I am ashamed to admit that my own family have tampered with the US elections, but what choice do I have? If my cousin succeeds he might charm Daisy away from me and not even my Phantom Duck persona will be enough to get her back.

Vaki Kokkinaki's Biography

I am a female Greek geek. I studied history and archaeology and I read almost everything. I am very fond of fairy tales and stories for children. I love writing in English but I have no idea why.

55: PAINTING

by Nam Raj Khatri

Inspired by: "Amy Sherald on painting Michelle Obama and being a first" by Anonymous, *Time*

There was an unsatisfied need in the mind of Nika. She wanted to be an artist and paint the people she saw around her. This interest surfaced when she visited an art gallery with her parents at the age of five.

The interest remained in her mind. She became busy with formal education. After college, she really started practicing. She developed quickly. She experimented, drawing the faces of people and trying to show a hidden happiness in their countenance.

One day, Nika saw a woman. She was looking beautiful, innocent and a little sad. She painted, modifying to bring hidden happiness, and changed the face. It looked gorgeous. She worked on it in minute detail, taking almost a year.

She displayed her artwork at an exhibition in a city gallery. People liked it very much. After the exhibition, there was a lot of demand for her artwork. Nika sold her painting for 200 million. Nika found the subject of the painting and provided her half the money. That brought real happiness to her face.

Nam Raj Khatri's Biography

Nam Raj Khatri, resident of Nepal. I am an environmental engineer also interested in artwork, singing and writing stories.

56: ART, BUT NOT AS HE KNEW IT

by Glen Donaldson

Inspired by: "A portrait created by AI just sold for $432,000. But is it really art?" by Jonathan Jones, *The Guardian*

Summoning every bit of his severe intelligence, Guy finally spoke. "If there's one thing I hate, it's ridiculous attempts at AI expressionism. And you can forget cultural bona fides. This painting is an evolutionary cul-de-sac, a Darwinian twilight zone, if you will. To hell with it passing the Turing test. It's plain to see. The thing's got no damn soul."

Guy was melancholic by nature. As he stood alone and muttered to himself, casting judgement within the floor-to-ceiling glass walls of the state-funded Petaflops Algorithm Museum of Contemporary Art in downtown Munich — the world's first gallery devoted wholly to showcasing computer-made artworks — the somewhat depressing and off-centre occasion was certainly no watershed moment for him. Beret-wearing Guy was a person comfortable in his own misery. You could tell.

The female security guard had begun staring arrows in his direction. He sensed his time was up. On his way out, he took the opportunity for one last derision.

"This goddamn machine art is all flapdoodle, but in an interesting way," he said to no one in particular.

Glen Donaldson's Biography

Glen Donaldson acknowledges roses and apples are related. He cites his all-time favourite movie as *The Man in the Gray Flannel Suit* starring Gregory Peck. Glen blogs weekly and uniquely at both *Scenic Writer's Shack* and *Lost In Space Fireside*.

www.goosefleshsite.wordpress.com

57: RED CARD

by Jon Spencer

Inspired by: "Analysis: Vladimir Putin is about to gain control of Interpol, the world's main law enforcement organization" by Vladimir Kara-Murza, *National Post*

"It's just a card, Mr President. Some kind of red playing card."

"Who's it from?" the president demanded.

"Doesn't say." The aide flipped the envelope over. "Postmark Lyon."

"Well, read it."

"There's no writing on it, sir. Oh, wait, there's another card inside." The aide pulled out a plain white printed card.

"Looks like Russian, sir." The aide called out to the room, "Who here reads Russian?"

"I read some." Bolton stepped forward and took the card.

"Ty dvigayesh'sya, ya igrayu," said Bolton.

"Meaning?" said the president.

"Roughly translated: you move, I play."

"Play what?"

The aide stepped forward, taking the card from Bolton.

"The card, sir. One false move, they play the card."

"A card? What do I care?"

The aide looked nervously at Bolton.

"A 'red card' is a red notice, an arrest warrant. From Interpol."

"So what?" said the president petulantly.

"Well, he runs it now."

Jon Spencer's Biography

Jon Spencer works in non-profits and writes fiction, screenplays and fantasy business plans. He has written and edited for Thomson Reuters and runs a writers group out of the back room of a Toronto teashop.

58: TURBULENCE

by Josie Gowler

Inspired by: "Ravenshoe wind turbine goes up in flames" by Anonymous, *Cairns Post*

Bobby whimpered. I bent down and scratched behind his ears. "I don't like thunderstorms, either," I muttered. The wind threw sand into my eyes and I turned seawards, pulling my long hair away from my face.

And that's when it happened, a massive arc of lightning streaking down and hitting one of the wind turbines off the coast. The ground shuddered. The creaking noise was audible even above the rain and ferocious wind. With a wrench of concrete and metal, water heaving and crashing, the turbines pulled their way out of the sea and towards land, like a row of pogo sticks bent on destruction.

Beach huts broke like matchsticks under them as they marched inland.

One bounded past so close that a massive cloud of damp sand showered over where we were cowering behind a dune. I turned to Bobby. "I told them that adding AI to the engine management system was a bad idea," I said. Except – being an accountant – I had argued against it on the grounds of cost.

Obviously, no one could have foreseen *this*.

Josie Gowler's Biography

Josie Gowler has had short stories published in *365 Tomorrows*, *Every Day Fiction*, *Ethereal Tales*, *Theaker's Quarterly Fiction*, *Aphelion* and *Perihelion*. Her specialties are weird tales set in the East Anglian Fens and science fiction and fantasy short stories.

59: RESIGNED TO IT

by Gary McGrath

Inspired by: "Melania Trump says she could be 'the most bullied person' in world" by AP, *The Guardian*

"You said you had a question?"

"Oh. Yeah. You know how you're, like, 'the most bullied person in the world'. Is that because of who you're married to?"

"What's that supposed to mean?"

"I mean, like, does he bully you? Or do other people bully you because of him? I'm just curious... that's all."

The first lady looked stunned.

The second lady continued, "I mean. He yells at everyone. He even yells when he's typing."

The first lady was about to react with an angry riposte, but she stayed silent for a heartbeat. Soft water flushed her eyes, gently. "He never used to be this way, you know. When we first met he was kind and gentle. He never yelled at all."

The second lady smiled, sympathetically. "People change when they're under pressure. Some people duck out of the responsibility. Others let it get to them and become aggressive."

"Well," said the first lady, sighing. "It looks like I'm stuck with it." She smiled a resigned smile and continued, "Because I would never expect to see Donald duck."

VOLUME 1

Gary McGrath's Biography

Freelance writer and commentator on life. Aspiring to greater things, through a love of language. Only just finding my voice in my fifties, but determined to be heard.

60: YOUR CALL IS IMPORTANT TO US

by Dee La Vardera

Inspired by: "Denzel: the sniffer dog that detects water leaks" by Nick Garnett, *BBC*

"Hello, hello, I have... I have a..." Marjorie is panicking.

"Wellness Water Company, here to help."

"I need to... need to..."

"Your call is important to us. Please listen to the following information so that we can direct your call to the appropriate department."

"I want... to... report..." Marjorie is worried about the pool of water under her feet, getting bigger by the minute.

"Please press 1 for an update on engineering works in your area, 2 for road closures for pipe-laying, 3 for accounts, 4 for water charges, 5 to change supplier, 6 for funny coloured water, 7 for smelly water, 8 for strange noises coming from your pipes or 9 to borrow a dog."

Marjorie cannot remember any of the numbers and what they stand for, so she stabs number 9. All she wants is to speak to a real human being. The phone bleeps and crackles and goes quiet.

"Hello, are you still there?"

"Press 1 for Alsatian, 2 for Labrador, 3 for Dachshund or 4 for Bichon Frise."

She needs her wellington boots now.

Dee La Vardera's Biography

Dee La Vardera is a writer and photographer from Wiltshire. Born a Brummie, now transformed into a Moonraker, she lives near a white horse cut into chalk downland, Silbury Hill and Avebury Stone Circle. Magical, mysterious and monumental surroundings.
www.dewfall-hawk.com

61: MATTIE

by Valerie Fish

Inspired by: "Trans activists send out free breast binders to 13-year-olds in unmarked packages... so their parents don't find out" by Sanchez Manning, *Mail on Sunday*

My name is Mattie and I hate my boobs. They remind me of who I am and who I don't want to be.

The package arrived today, in plain brown paper just as they'd promised. Mum was out anyway, so I escaped the inevitable interrogation.

She wouldn't understand, couldn't understand, would more than likely say, "It's just a phase."

I took the package up to my room, grateful that I would be undisturbed for a while.

I pulled the garment over my breasts. I'm not particularly well endowed in that area, but anything is too much for me.

It felt tight against my chest, pulling everything downwards. How on earth was I going to be able to breathe? But hey, no pain, no gain.

"Mattie, I'm home.

"Mattie, are you up there?"

I heard her footsteps up the stairs. There was nothing I could do to stop her. She barged in without knocking as per usual, took one look at me and went as white as a sheet.

That'll teach her to knock in future.

Valerie Fish's Biography

Valerie has had a love of the English language since her school days, inspired by a fantastic English teacher. She likes to 'write from the heart' and hopes that's reflected in her work.

62: A FAULTY GUIDE FOR THE BLEARY-EYED

by Amanda Garzia

Inspired by: "Valsartan from Mylan laboratories in India can no longer be used in EU medicines due to NDEA impurity" by Anonymous, *European Medicines Agency*

"Asthma? Never. My liver? Could easily be mistaken for a 40-year-old's."

Dr Hill grabbed a green prescription form.

Tom's grip on his cane relaxed. This GP was taking his word for it. Not even a cursory tap on the chest. He had to hand it to his brother, this had really been a cinch.

True, he'd taken three buses in holiday traffic, spent ages in line. But tonight, courtesy of modern medicine, he'd sleep for the first time in a week. Ever since, in fact, his son's family had invaded the house, there to stay until New Year's.

He couldn't wait to conk out. To sleep in heavenly peace, oblivious to baby Jay's crying.

Joyful and triumphant, Tom hobbled to the pharmacy, waving his prescription at the chemist. Barely 10 minutes until closing time.

"I'm terribly sorry, sir, but this is out of stock."

"Is there a late-night dispensary nearby?"

"Oh, you won't be able to find it anywhere. It's been recalled. What with the seasonal chaos and all, it's anybody's guess when it will be back on the shelves."

Amanda Garzia's Biography

At age 12, Amanda typed the first edition of her own (now defunct) magazine, posting copies to Canadian friends left behind on coming to Malta. Having written for the *Times of Malta*, *Pink*, and *Child*, she's presently concentrating on fiction.

63: DRONING ON

by Len Saculla

Inspired by: "Gatwick runway reopens after drone chaos" by Anonymous, *BBC*

"It's another drone problem. Coordinated to attack major airports and clog up airspace right across northern and western Europe. Terrorists. Or idiots."

"You can't stop me flying, young man. I have important work to do."

"So do loads of people, Granddad. We've got top surgeons who can't get to their fee-paying hospitals to operate on social media celebrities. With live podcasts having to be cancelled. So don't tell me how important YOU are."

"The government – all governments – should be better prepared. It's nearly Christmas, an exceptionally busy time of the year."

"Tell me about it. Now, listen, you'd best turn around and head off home and follow BBC World Service." There seemed to be no choice.

The team of elves were shocked and disappointed when Santa Claus brought his sleigh home early. And still fully laden.

Mrs Santa was furious. "Let me unpack," she insisted.

Soon she had two piles. One of pristine boxes... and one of unwrapped gifts ready for the hammer.

"These children have been naughty, not nice," she said. "No drones for them this Christmas."

Len Saculla's Biography

Len Saculla has appeared in several previous challenges set by Christopher Fielden. He has also been published online at the science fiction and horror flash site *Speculative 66*, along with appearances in *Kind of a Hurricane Press* anthologies.

64: NEW HORIZONS – ULTIMA THULE

by Gavin Biddlecombe

Inspired by: "NASA's New Horizons Mission Reveals Entirely New Kind of World" by Anonymous, *NASA*

The President strode into the conference room, speaking before reaching the podium. The gathered reporters hushed.

"I appreciate you all for coming in from your New Year celebrations to mark this historic occasion," he said.

"You're leaving?" asked one of the reporters.

The President checked his agenda. "No, I don't think so."

"Right. Excuse my interruption."

The President looked around at the expectant faces before proceeding. "We've received news from NASA that New Horizons has sent back the first detailed images of Ultima Thule from the Kuiper Belt, the furthest object ever explored in our solar system. Whilst promising, this also comes with worrying news for future space exploration and any attempts to land on this object."

"Mr President," said another reporter, standing up. "Surely NASA can manage this considering the ESA landed the Rosetta spacecraft on comet 67P."

"Well, yes and no."

Around the room, an unsettled murmur began.

"Please," he urged, "let me continue. Whilst landing may be possible, it appears from our images that their immigration policy is even more stringent than ours."

Gavin Biddlecombe's Biography

Gavin lives in Gibraltar with his wife and crazy little dog. He spends his free time reading, writing and working on his photography. He has several writing projects on the go and hopes to see them in print.

www.gavinbiddlecombe.wordpress.com

65: JUSTICE FOR PIERS MORGAN

by Jacob Weller

Inspired by: "ROLL WITH IT Piers Morgan reveals he was hospitalised with gastritis and blames vegan sausage rolls" by Dan Cain, *The Sun*

Twitter. The best place to get news. None of that lefty rubbish on there if you follow the right people. People like Piers Morgan, they know best. They talk sense most of the time. He knows what's up, unlike communist Corbyn or foolish Diane Abbott. He knows it all. That's why I believe him when he talks. He makes sense to me. Like when he said nobody needed that vegan sausage roll. It's a shambles, honestly. The meat industry is one of the things that this country was built on. Proper British bacon, chicken, lamb chops and pork scratchings. Sausages. Big, fat and juicy ones. This stuff at Greggs needs to stop. Tomorrow morning I'm gonna buy all the proper sausage rolls and make sure everybody remembers what a proper one tastes like.

I've bought the lot from Greggs. All 30. Gave them out on the street. Everybody's going to love them. Might just eat a few myself.

I haven't left the bathroom in three hours. But these are still better than that vegan rubbish. It was well worth it.

VOLUME 1

Jacob Weller's Biography

Jacob is a 25-year-old working in publishing. He lives in Cambridge and enjoys Dungeons & Dragons, baking and stroking every cat he comes across on the street.
www.linkedin.com/in/jacob-weller-58732760/

66: IMPEACH HIM

by Yvonne Mallett

Inspired by: "Trump is told tantrums are no solution to wall stand-off" by Alan Fram, *Metro*

In a dramatic move, the Down-to-Earth party today blocked their leader's plans to introduce agricultural boundaries between members' plots.

Insults flew in the bitter debate and leader, Butternut Squash, in tantrum mode, warned he would close all distribution routes and introduce trade tariffs.

First, Butternut Squash tackled the Brussels sprouts, calling them up tight, too green for politics and in cahoots with the Swedes, accusing them of criminal infiltration and cybercrime on behalf of foreign powers. And when the ginger plants brought even more heat to the debate, calling Butternut too old and going soft and yellow on top, "Ginger, you're barmy," was his bellowing reply.

Turnips and potatoes took a harder line in their deep-rooted defiance. "The land must produce and share its bounty. We will not be moved."

"I will withhold all fertilisers," screamed Butternut. "Call it a boundary, or a barrier if you will, but you will not flourish on the wrong side of the border."

And to shouts of approval the cry went up from the soft fruits, "Impeach him, impeach him."

VOLUME 1

Yvonne Mallett's Biography

I started working life as a reporter on a local paper in Ilford, subsequently worked as (among a number of other things) a freelance journalist, a press officer and copywriter.

67: MIKE OSCAR ZERO

by David McTigue

Inspired by: "Screen Actors Guild accuses Academy of 'intimidation' over Oscars ceremony" by Anonymous, *The Guardian*

"Hi, Mike, how's it goin'?"

I look up from my security radio set. "Good, thank you sir."

Wade Poundstone, nominated for best actor, saunters in and smiles like an electric strip light.

Next is Tanya Hyde, a dumb limey actress. By the look of her dress, she's won a couple of Golden Globes already. Dafter – I mean BAFTA – nominated, she probably thinks Hamlet is a small pig.

I've been head of this watch for years. Security is king.

Word is I'll be getting a lifetime award. Must remember to thank God. Jeez, there's probably an award for best clapperboard.

All in now, thank God.

Looking round, I figure the combined cost of this gig, and the wealth of these people, could clear the debt of a small country, or get some homeless people accommodation.

All this for dressing up and playing Let's Pretend like my grandkids do. Plastic people in Tinseltown.

Guess it's time to get my lifetime award, so pardon me while I load this semi-automatic pistol.

Mike Oscar Zero, over and out.

David McTigue's Biography

Lives on outskirts of Liverpool. Married, three demons, one lovely grandson. Published in various magazines over thirty years ago, now trying to get back into the swing of writing. Flash fiction helps a lot.

68: TAKE BACK CONTROL

by Lucy Morrice

Inspired by: "No-deal Brexit puts UK food security at risk, warn Sainsbury's, Asda, Waitrose and M&S" by Ben Chapman, *The Independent*

She grubbed in the wet clay soil and brought up a sad specimen or two. Wrinkled onions and carrots, not getting any bigger, however much she tried to grow green fingers. Her potatoes were doing well, but she only had a few large pots with those, hardly enough to feed three hungry teenagers.

"Bit like the siege of Leningrad," she grimly remarked to herself, wondering how long it would be before they were reduced to eating handbags, shoes and leather bound books. Or the cat.

"At least we have control now," she sneered. "We can make choices; whose turn it is to have breakfast today, whose turn to empty the toilet bucket. And I always fancied an early retirement, although I hadn't visualised it being quite like this. We are lucky to live in a village," she admitted. "We do have some community spirit and at least we are all in it together."

Lucy Morrice's Biography

Lucy has high hopes of being a published writer one day, but she is easily distracted by almost anything when settling down to write. Flash fiction is her favourite invention.

69: TIME CRITICAL

by Paul Mastaglio

Inspired by: "The geezer guaranteed to win: Actor Ray Winstone fronts bet365 adverts profiting off punters' bad fortune... no wonder his own daughter is horrified" by Guy Adams, *Daily Mail*

The smart television presenter faced the camera. "Dan Jones," he purred. "I bring you lucky viewers your best opportunity yet." He stepped back from the lens.

Revealed on screen were two musclebound men holding aloft identical weights. From the side, his voice continued, "All you have to do is register which one of these competitors will last the longest and the time difference, in minutes and seconds, between the two efforts. It's 10 pounds a go. If you guess correctly, you win 100,000 pounds. Go on, you know you want to."

Watching at home was one Jeremiah Johnston. He was resplendent in purple trousers and flowered shirt. Gold bracelets dangled from his wrists as he waved them at Winston, sitting next to him on the couch.

"Who's it going to be then, love?" Jeremiah pointed at the screen. "This one?" No response. "That one?" Winston woofed. "You picked me. I knew you would. After all, I am your daddy."

"Woof," agreed Winston.

"Now, if I could just remember how long I lasted after the other fellow..."

Paul Mastaglio's Biography

Retired bank clerk who lives with wife, Yvonne, in North Tyneside with our cat, Toby. Interests include archery, reading and walking.

70: ALL THE TRIMMINGS: AN APPETIZING STORY FOR ENTREPRENEURS EVERYWHERE

by K. J. Watson

Inspired by: "Cooking roast dinner produces air pollution as bad as heavily polluted city streets, study reveals" by Josh Gabbatiss, *The Independent*

When governments worldwide banned roast dinners to protect the environment, the entrepreneur Bob Uroncle acted fast.

Bob launched a range of roast dinner scents. He offered candles, drawer liners, air fresheners and perfume. Each of these exuded the smell of a roast beef dinner with all the trimmings. Within weeks, Bob was a billionaire.

Bob missed a trick, though. Governments had included non-meat roast meals in their ban. Vegetarians and vegans protested that the basis of all Bob's products was roast beef. They demanded scents which captured the aroma of a nut roast dinner.

Bob's own carnivorous lifestyle may have clouded his judgement. He ignored the anti-meat lobbyists. Another entrepreneur, Jack Nory, spotted an opportunity. Jack's 'nut roast dinner and all the appropriate trimmings' scents were a hit.

Following Jack's success, Bob admitted his error. He sold his scent business to Jack and consulted a lawyer about the limits of the international roast dinner law. He then bought a space shuttle and converted a disused space station into a restaurant. Bob's out-of-this-world roast dinners (with vegetarian and vegan options) proved a goldmine. Bob had done it again.

K. J. Watson's Biography

I am a copy editor and online content writer. My occasional fiction includes scripts for a comic and annual (some while ago) and stories for young children. I live near Loch Lomond with my wife and two dogs.

71: SHE WAS JUST BACK HOME

by Simon Williams

Inspired by: "Shamima Begum: IS teenager to lose UK citizenship" by Anonymous, *BBC*

She was just back, just back home. After years away, the world she had known looked different and people looked at her differently. She had changed too, of course, you could see that in her eyes, if she ever allowed you to look into them.

She was asleep and flinching in dreams when the window broke. The half-brick hit the cot and glass showered across the room. She screamed and screamed as she picked glass from her baby's face. Her father ran into the room, face pale, eyes wild. He saw blood on his grandson's head.

She went to the funeral, of course she did. He was her father, her son's grandfather. Dressed in black, she stood next to her mother in the grey mist and rain. Together they raised their eyes to the sky and the rain mixed with their silent tears. Tomorrow they would move away, the woman, the girl and her boy, move far away from their home, move to a place where their past was not known, where the past did not shadow their lives.

Simon Williams' Biography

Simon lives and works in Edinburgh, where he writes and runs. You can read more of his writing at:
www.simonsalento.com

72: DAWNING OF THE NEW AGE PHILOSOPHY

by Maggie Elliott

Inspired by: "STEPHEN GLOVER: Why, with a heavy heart, I fear Prince Harry may be riding for a fall" by Steven Glover, *Daily Mail*

Strange looks were exchanged as Meg and Harold confirmed they intended to raise their child gender neural, a vegetarian and with a male nanny.

The clatter of dishes and distance from head to foot of the dining table didn't prevent their patriarch's scorn being heard. "New Age claptrap," he snapped.

He was silenced by a wave of hand from the matriarch who demanded, "Enough. Let's eat."

As Meg went into labour, a delivery suite was prepared as per her instructions.

Tranquil sounds, soft lighting and hypnotherapy helped initially, but as the contractions lengthened and deepened, so did Meg's grip on her husband's hand.

As the pain became continuous and extreme, her attempt to negate it with the techniques she had learned, failed, as did her resolve. It dawned on her that accepting medical intervention was not a sign of weakness, nor did it demean her philosophy.

Pain relief administered, a healthy gender-neutral baby arrived whose nursery was decorated with nontoxic, organic, vegan paint, infused with eucalyptus oil to enhance memory, boost the immune system and stimulate creativity.

Maggie Elliott's Biography

Maggie is retired and writes purely for pleasure. Her first poem 'Picture Me Calm' won third prize in the *Writing Magazine* poetry competition in 2018.

73: PATTY BRIDAL

by Chris Green

Inspired by: "Award success for Ivory Bridal Suite" by Daniel Laurie, *South Wales Guardian*

"This is it, we're here."

The two women came to a stop outside the boutique and gazed at the window display.

"Oh Mum, the dresses are gorgeous. I want to try them all," gasped the younger of the two.

"You know, Lisa, this is where I got my wedding dress from. 30 years ago now," explained her mother. She looked up at the shop's sign and frowned. "Mind you, it wasn't called Patty Bridal back then."

They both stepped inside and were treated to a wonderland of wedding dresses… and the smell of fried onions.

They looked at each other, puzzled.

From amongst the forest of satin a young man approached, wearing a chef's hat and a dirty apron.

"I understand the look on your faces," he laughed. "We have a burger stand at the far end of the shop."

"Really?"

"Yes, we do all kinds of burgers – cheeseburgers, chilli burgers, Hawaiian burgers, veggie burgers…"

Lisa clapped her hands in delight. "Forget the wedding dress, Mum," she said. "Let's get some burgers. I want to try them all."

VOLUME 1

Chris Green's Biography

Chris Green is a former accountant from the north west of England. He is a reader, an occasional writer and a failed singer. His interests include football, music hall and cheese.

74: LOST THE THREAD

by Mark J Towers

Inspired by: "My life sewing for a 15-inch 'diva'" by Anonymous, *BBC*

Vzzzzzt. Vzzzzzt.

Hal dreaded that sound. His phone was on silent but it startled him whenever it vibrated on his desk.

He read the text. *IS IT READY?*

Hal's fingers hovered over the screen. He considered replying with equivalent terseness, thought better of it and put the phone down.

He scanned the room. His discarded efforts strewn everywhere. Every suggestion had been slapped down in a string of caps lock characters.

Vzzzzzt. Vzzzzzt. Vzzzzzt. Vzzzzzt. Vzzzzzt. Vzzzzzt.

The phone jiggled for longer. No hiding from his impatient client.

He picked up the phone but the call ended.

Vzzzzzt. Vzzzzzt.

Another text. *WELL?*

Hal's fingers wiggled over the screen, touch-typing his response. *I have bit Andrew well being it tight now.*

His heart needled at the predictive text errors on the unsent text. Hal corrected it and tucked the phone in his pocket.

As he departed, he picked up the completed design. A sequinned gown, laced with gold thread, diamantes, pearls, the whole works.

If this design failed, Hal had designs on one more killer outfit this diva would die for.

Mark J Towers' Biography

Mark J Towers writes children's books, short stories, flash fiction and poetry whenever he has spare time from 'Dad-taxi' duties.

75: ROALD DAHL, WHOSE VERSES WERE CENSURED

by Gail Everett

Inspired by: "Aldi removes Roald Dahl's *Revolting Rhymes* from its Australian stores over the word 'slut'" by Elisa Criado, *The Independent*

Mr Dahl's *Revolting Rhymes*,
    Became a victim of the times,
    We live in. And the Aldi mob,
    Should go and get a decent job,
    Before they strip the shelves quite bare,
    It seems they simply have no care.
    Political correctness rules,
    In supermarkets, shops and schools,
    So customers will walk away,
    In anger, Aldi now must pay,
    The price, in loss of revenue,
    From selling less to me and you.
    The moral of this story is,
    That ignorance is seldom bliss.

Gail Everett's Biography

Apart from what I told my mother when I was a teenager, my interest in fiction began at the tender age of 63, by which time I had exhausted most other possibilities for pastimes in which to engage whilst sitting down.

76: SELF-IDENTITY VS. LABELS

by Raymond E. Strawn III

Inspired by: "#NotMyAriel: White Twitter Is Big Mad About Disney Casting a Black Little Mermaid" by Michael Harriot, *The Root*

During dinner, a family discussed a movie they'd seen.

"Who's your favourite character?" the father asked his child.

"The main character," the child shouted in joy.

"A good choice," the mother said.

"I want to grow up and be the main character."

"Oh, little one, you can't. That's impossible."

"But why, Daddy?" the child asked.

"Because you're different. You don't look like they do."

"That doesn't make sense, Daddy. In church, Jesus is white, but he's really middle eastern, so I can be whoever I want."

The mother spat her wine.

"We don't talk like that. Do you understand?" The father scowled.

"I don't, Daddy. You say I can't be the main character because I'm different. Jesus is portrayed as white, but he is middle eastern. Why can't I portray the main character if I'm different?"

"Enough." The father slammed his fist into the table. "You can't be that person, do *you* understand."

"No, Daddy. *You* don't understand. I can be *whoever* I want." The child left the table.

Raymond E. Strawn III's Biography

Raymond E. Strawn III began writing poetry and short stories in 1999. In 2001-2002, he spent 48 days wrongfully incarcerated for writing and sharing his poetry and short stories at his high school.

77: SO MUCH FOR THE BORIS BOUNCE

by Kenneth Muir

Inspired by: "Tories hope the 'Boris Bounce' can save them in Brecon: Voters go to the polls in crucial by-election that could slash Johnson's majority to ONE as he faces first big test against Lib Dems and Brexit Party" by James Tapsfield, *Mail Online*

Charlie worked all week, canvassing the neighbourhood, extolling the virtues of voting Conservative in the coming by-election.

He enjoyed the rising sun that beautiful summer day, as he cheerfully strode down the street on his way to his watering hole. Everyone he met along the way smiled or greeted him.

The night before, he was inebriated and failed to follow the election results. That morning, in the bath, he sang a song he'd made up loudly, to the tune of ABBA's 'Money, Money, Money': "Boris, Boris, Boris, is our man."

In a cheerful voice, he ordered his lager.

The pub landlord asked, "Why so gleeful."

"Because the Tories will win the by-election for sure. Boris is our man."

Later, his soul mate, Allan, arrived. He said, in a mournful groan, "The Tories lost."

Charlie was crestfallen. His face became red with anger and he strolled around shouting, punching the air. The other patrons whispered in fear.

What triggered him off – made him so cross – was the *Daily Mail*'s screaming headline, shown on Charlie's laptop: 'So much for the Boris Bounce'.

Kenneth Muir's Biography

My name is Kenneth Muir, married, British nationality, living in the Philippines since 1987. I chose short story writing as a therapy in my old age. I am 83 years old this year.

78: TIPPING POINTS

by Bridget Scrannage

Inspired by: "School strike for climate: Protests staged around the world" by Anonymous, *BBC*

"OK class – if you're going to go on climate strike and skip my lessons, I want to be sure you understand what you are protesting about and not just skiving. This is an old-fashioned balance scale. It works by putting a known weight, in this case 100 grams, in one of the brass pans and then balancing a substance on the opposite side until they're level. I'll use coal to represent CO2 producing fossil fuels. The known weight represents the natural world." The teacher put in pieces of coal until the scales were level. "Can anyone tell me what effect it will have if I add more coal?"

"Global warming."

"Rising sea levels."

"Correct. Yes."

"Mrs Wright gets naked."

"What?" The teacher stared at the speaker, a young girl not known for her insolence.

"She says climate change is rubbish and she'll streak through the school if it happens."

"Your headmistress said that?"

The class agreed.

He thought of his boss, shuddered and resolved to go green.

Bridget Scrannage's Biography

Bridget Scrannage is a writer with a passion for sustainability. She's the founder of a large global writing community. Her work has been published online and in numerous anthologies.
   www.bridgetscrannage.wordpress.com

79: SENSELESS KILLING

by Hajra Saeed

Inspired by: "Elephant ears and lion bones among hunting trophies imported into the UK" by Patrick Greenfield, *The Guardian*

My 12 year old son and I were having breakfast one day when he suddenly asked me, "Mum, do you think my children will get to see elephants, lions and rhinos?"

Momentarily taken aback, I slowly set down my mug of tea and asked, "Whatever made you say that?"

"Well, I have been reading online how 'human beings' are exterminating wild animals by the thousands and I don't think there will be any left in the next 15 years or so."

"Oh," was all I said.

"Did you know that every day 100 elephants lose their lives for ivory, meat and body parts? While approximately only 25,000 to 40,000 wild lions remain worldwide, mostly because trophy hunters just kill them for fun."

"No, I didn't," I replied.

"And rhinos might become extinct in a few years because their horns are considered a symbol of wealth and power. What is wrong with us? How can we be so cruel? When will this stop?"

I sat there staring at him, for I had no answers.

Hajra Saeed's Biography

Hajra Saeed has been writing for 22 years in Pakistan. Her work has been published in many leading newspapers and magazines there. Currently, she is working as a web-based creative writer and editor. She loves to read and take online courses.

80: JALLAD IS WAITING

by Majella Pinto

Inspired by: "Nirbhaya case: Four Indian men executed for 2012 Delhi bus rape and murder" by Anonymous, *Yahoo*

Seven long years...
 Has it been that long?
 Just yesterday I had read the horrific account of the defiled Med with details gory.
 Has justice been delivered?
 The Encounter under the bridge for another Med was swift and fair.
 Where hides that juvenile disguised under the loophole in law?
 Law that protects the one who maimed without protecting its own honour?
 Find him, find him,
 It is his blood I thirsts for,
 Justice isn't done, my thirst isn't quenched,
 Five lives for one, what more do you want?
 I want every life for that one,
 A life that wasn't revered.
 She was in the wrong place at the wrong time.
 I wish none of this to ever happen,
 Not to her, not to any, never, never, never.
 Then, justice will be done.
 Give me the blood of that last one.
 Jallad is waiting.

Majella Pinto's Biography

Majella Pinto, raised in India, is an artist and writer based in California. She works in Silicon Valley and is devoutly focused on her twin passions of art and literature.

81: IT WAS AN ORDINARY TUESDAY

by Madeleine Fox

Inspired by: "Mark Wahlberg movie turns Cardiff Street into US action scene" by Thomas Deacon, *Wales Online*

Llandaff fields were autumnally beautiful. Crisp orange leaves crunching under foot and pram. Baby Mari snuggly sleeping.

Murmurings in the queue at the park's café: What's going on? Terrorists?

The inside full of police, she perched on a low wall outside. "Your grandchild?" asked a woman with coffee cup balanced on the cycle helmet in her lap.

"Yes, I—"

"I've got two. I don't do that childcare nonsense."

"No. Well—"

"What's all this?" The woman indicated the seven parked police cars and vans obstructing paths and damaging grass. And without waiting for a reply, "They should sort out the lot living opposite me. Young men affording a house like that. Foreign, if you take my meaning. And they never look you in the eye."

"Well, I'd better get the baby home." Turning sharply, she ran the pram into a tall uniformed man.

A familiar yet unfamiliar deep voice, "Sorry."

Multi-tasking pram and phone she texted, *Home soon. Just ran into an actor from The Bill.*

Madeleine Fox's Biography

Madeleine is a former special needs teacher who turns her hand to writing when not painting in her studio.

82: DRINKING THE PUB DRY

by Alan Barker

Inspired by: "Coronavirus: Goats take over empty streets of seaside town" by Anonymous, *BBC*

Joe could hardly believe the carnage that greeted him on returning to work following the virus lockdown.

It had been a horrible few months having to close the pub indefinitely and his beloved wife, Flo, walking out, leaving him home alone.

He gazed round the pub at the animals – meerkats, monkeys, pandas, gorillas and many more – sprawled across the floor, slumped in seats, some clutching spirit bottles, others sleeping like the dead with tongues hanging out. How the beer-swilling elephant had got in was anyone's guess.

A giraffe sporting dark glasses was propping up the bar. Joe stepped over a prone crocodile and said, "Shouldn't you lot be in the zoo?"

The giraffe sipped something fizzy and replied, "We fancied going out on a jolly and when we saw the sign 'The Fursty Ferret', we thought it was a watering hole for animals. Bad move."

A door behind the bar opened and Flo appeared.

"What are you doing here?" Joe demanded.

"Just going with the flow and self-isolating. Here," she said, passing Joe a broom. "You can start clearing up."

Alan Barker's Biography

Alan, a retired tax accountant, lives within a horse's gallop of Epsom Racecourse and is a season ticket holder at Woking FC (sadly). He enjoys writing daft stories which occasionally get published when he cuts out the silly speling misteaks.

83: THE BINS REBELLION CRASHES THE RUBBISH PARTY

by Antonio Salituro

Inspired by: "'I haven't laughed so much in my life': the Australians dressing up to celebrate bin night" by Katie Cunningham, *The Guardian*

"Your 30th birthday celebration will be grander than The Royal Easter show in Sydney," Tyler exclaimed.

"I want an eco-friendly party," Naomi warned him.

"I'll get some more bins," he replied.

Naomi frowned at her boyfriend, without saying a word.

The night had finally come. Their garden was packed with people, yet their bins were overloaded with rubbish.

"Where are the glasses?" Naomi asked.

"Have some mojito, it's delicious," Tyler said.

"I don't want to drink from a plastic cup. Told you to buy more glasses, didn't I?" she snapped.

"Got plenty of bins... hang on, where have they gone?" he gasped.

Suddenly, everyone started screaming and running away. A gang of furious bins were spitting garbage out onto the party guests.

"Who's in charge?" Ro-bin, the leader of the filthy rebellion, asked.

"Naomi," Tyler said, hidden behind a bush.

"Sorry, it's my birthday, I'll clean this mess," Naomi said, blushing.

"Environment deserves respect, and so do you," Ro-bin said, helping Naomi pick up the waste.

Then he quelled the bins' rage, while Naomi's rose up against Tyler.

Antonio Salituro's Biography

I am an early stage freelance writer and the pieces I have written so far are mostly non-fictional (e.g. documentaries, articles). However, I have recently got into writing fictional short stories (including flash fiction) as well as poetry.

84: NO, NOT ME

by Ashutosh Pant

Inspired by: "Red Cross disinfecting streets on Day 24 of coronavirus lockdown" by Anonymous, *The Himalayan Times*

"What happened to me?" I shouted loudly.

I'd had a dream about turning into a car and it has happened to me in real-life. I was a car.

I tried to turn on my engine. No, it wouldn't start.

From far away, I saw Red Cross workers disinfecting vehicles. I tried to run, but my engine still refused to power on.

When they came near me, I had to run. So, I removed the stone that was stopping me and I fled quickly, into the darkness of the night.

Ashutosh Pant's Biography

My name is Ashutosh Pant. I study in class 7. I am 13 years old.

85: A WIN-WIN DEAL

by Matilda Pinto

Inspired by: "Monkeys take over hotel, become tourists & swim all day amid COVID-19 outbreak" by Ebenezer Quist, *Yen*

'Monkeys take over hotel and swim all day.' Quirky yet incredible. Hats off to the monkeys who took advantage of the lockdown to go swimming in that pricey pool, all for free.

The horde of elephants in China did better. They slept at a tea garden with honeyed smiles on their faces, drunk on corn wine, with no care in the world.

Seems like the world order is about to change in a direction man has no control over. What if the animals take over the planet, take advantage of the pandemonium and keep men out of sight? Not viable demonstrated Orwell.

Is that an option at all?

Never overlook the depressed pigeons looking for clusters of tourists who fed them day after day at St Mark's Square and the Kabootar Khana.

The pigeons want us around. So do the elephants, to grow corn for the wine, and the monkeys will surely revert to their forested habitat if it is not violated.

Folks, the way out of the current predicament is a world for all and all for the world.

Matilda Pinto's Biography

Among Matilda's not so favourite things is 'discrimination'. Instances of social, gender, religious, national and other discrimination upset her. The latest virus is a great teacher. "It does not choose," she says. Matilda is a novelist and short story writer.

www.facebook.com/matilda.pinto.9

86: KITTY ON THE LOOSE

by Benjamin Noel

Inspired by: "Reports That Tiger Was Released From Oakland Zoo During Protests Appear To Be Part Of A Viral Hoax" by Nathan Francis, *Inquisitr*

Last week, accounts of an escaped big cat shook the San Francisco Bay. Within minutes, the shared attitude of the area changed from the blithe to a rather frightened aloofness. And my household was no exception.

The carefree idiosyncratic atmosphere in the room suddenly changed, for fear of an imminent tiger attack, as our animalistic response kicked in. As there are not many places a human can fly on their own, we opted to fight, arming ourselves with every bat, club and shield we could fashion. Armed with bamboo sticks, couch pillows and frying pans, we felt prepared to face the beast, huddled in formation in the living room, ready for a furry intruder from any direction.

But, after holding our modern day phalanx for an hour, eyes fell low, and muscles lax. But then, after a scrutinous look at his phone, my jubilant brother jumped up and exclaimed, "It was all just a joke," and the anxiety of dealing with a rather unfriendly kitten left the household just as quickly as it came.

Benjamin Noel's Biography

News of a tiger on the loose provided me just enough motivation to write something during this otherwise stagnant time.

87: THE REAL STORY

by Tiffany H White

Inspired by: "Llamas deliver food packages to people self-isolating in Wales" by Harry Cockburn, *The Independent*

"Have you seen the news?"

"Gagh."

"Did I wake you? Sorry. I thought you were working."

"Same thing."

"Apparently. So, you haven't seen the news?"

"Let me guess – a pandemic perhaps? The end of civilisation? Meghan Markle is gay? No, I haven't seen the news. Why should I?"

"Not everything is about you."

"Well, actually, it is. Definition of self-isolation."

"You're an idiot. We're out of milk."

"Can you get me some fags when you go?"

"No."

"I didn't expect the end of the world to be so boring. Not a zombie in sight. At least, not yet. I can only live in hope."

"Come and watch the news with me. Might cheer you up."

"Best not. No news is good news."

"Not always. Get up. I'll draw the curtains, let in some light."

"Oh my god, I can see the gnus."

"Told you."

Tiffany H White's Biography

Ms White currently identifies as a single white female in her late fifties with anti-social media disorder.

88: TRUTH UNCOVERED

by James Louis Peel

Inspired by: "Trump attacks his own CDC scientists over how to reopen schools safely" by Brett Murphy and Letitia Stein, *USA Today*

Sarah, the budding archaeologist of year 2892, heard the imaginary announcements of her discoveries being made into the year's best documentary on the deadly crisis and political upheaval of 2020.

Here, in the Orleans scrublands on Earth, it was perpetually dusty and 20 miles inland from the Gulf of the United States of Mexico. Sarah's team lead University of Crater Bay's first dig on the old home world. Coming from Mars, it was the pinnacle of a dream. She pulled her face filter tighter.

Many preserved events of 2020 in historic media were recorded clearly. But the mixed stories, unreliable truthfulness of the times and lack of verifiable material evidence made understanding difficult. Sarah's mind repeated, *The Third Dark Age started 872 years ago*. She imagined the interviews.

From remains of a Clintonian dynasty, thwarted by Obomians, culminating in little understood presidents, 300 years of a Dark Age began. Sarah searched for the name, was it 'Trimp' or 'Tramp'? No one knew. Now, Sarah was about to resolve that as a tip of a broken statue began to emerge.

James Louis Peel's Biography

James Louis Peel is a Kentuckian living in Japan. He writes about what he sees and enjoys sharing and learning from the wit and wisdom of all good friends and strange events in his life.

89: STRANGE MUTATIONS

by Peggy Gerber

Inspired by: "College Students, Cabo and the Coronavirus" by Gaby Galvin, *U.S. News*

"Honey, come quickly. You'll never believe this."

Jillian was just cracking the eggs for breakfast when she heard Ryan bellowing from the dining room. As she raced in, he thrust the newspaper at her shouting, "Check this out."

Jillian's eyes grew wide as she began reading, 'College Students, Mutating Virus, Forbidden Spring Break'. She looked at Ryan and said, "I can't believe they all got sick."

Ryan asked, "Did you read the paragraph yet where they discuss how the virus mutated? All 300 students had their noses and ears fall off. They just woke up with holes in their faces. Eww, look at the photos, those kids look like Porky Pig. Doctors don't know what happened, although one theory is the mutation occurred due to the amount of alcohol the students ingested."

Jillian sighed. "It's kind of an ironic twist that the kids that wouldn't wear masks will now have to wear prosthetic ones. So sad."

Ryan nodded his head in agreement, adding, "Honey, would you mind cooking some bacon this morning? I just got a hankering."

Peggy Gerber's Biography

Peggy Gerber is a poet and short story writer having been published in *Potato Soup Journal*, *Spillwords*, *Daily Science Fiction* and *101 Words*. Her hobbies include discussing Elmo and dinosaurs with her grandchildren, and writing for Chris Fielden's challenges.

90: THE FRUIT-FULL ARGUMENT

by A S Winter

Inspired by: "'Bullying' Apple fights couple over pear logo" by Natalie Sherman, *BBC*

The fruit market was noisy but an argument could be heard.

"Return my fruit," said one man.

"No, this is mine," replied another man.

A gentleman who had been watching them for a while decided to help them out. He requested they calm down and explain the problem.

The first man said, "He stole an apple from my fruit stall."

The second man said, "I am not a thief and it is not an apple."

The gentleman asked the second man, "Could you show me?"

The second man gave the fruit to the gentleman. It was a pear.

"Is this your apple?" the gentleman asked the first man.

"Yes," the first man replied.

"This is a pear," the gentleman said.

"Look at its shape. It is the same as an apple," said the first man.

"What colour are your apples?" the gentleman asked the first man.

"I don't check the colour of all of them, but this one was stolen from my stall because its colour is different."

This needs special attention, the gentleman thought. He called the police.

A S Winter's Biography

A S Winter uses his vivid imagination and creativity to write flash fictions and short stories. His work has been published in anthologies and on flash fiction websites. Currently, he is working on his first children's book.

91: TEARS OF BLACK

by Chris Lee

Inspired by: "Black employees describe systemic racism in the VA" by Nikki Wentling, *Stars and Stripes*

The doors rushed open, accompanied by the distant bark of orders. A blur of blue scrubs rushed by the inquisitive eyes in the hospital lobby. The glaring red words 'Operation in Progress' blared as the sound of clattering wheels diminished.

Parker barely made out a faint, dark figure holding his arm when he grew conscious. His surroundings perpetually spun, but eventually, things found their place in the room.

"Mr Parker?" a female voice inquired.

Parker winced as he looked up, but immediately flinched and pulled back his arm. His once groggy eyes were now filled with resentment and disgust. His eyes were drawn to the needle held in proximity to his arm. "I'd like to see a *real* doctor," he said flatly, looking away. The woman's eyebrows furrowed.

"Sir, I'm a medically trained professional and your medication—" she managed with a tremble in her voice.

Parker set his jaw, and refused to meet her eyes. The sight of the blur of blue scrubs returned as she hastily stepped out, the purpose and confidence drained from her body.

Chris Lee's Biography

Chris was born in New Jersey, but spent much of his life in Korea and Singapore. He is a high school junior at Singapore American School. An avid writer and voracious reader, he loves learning about politics, business and economics.

92: STORIES I NEVER WROTE

by Andrew Ball

Inspired by: "A university is offering scholarships for you to do absolutely nothing" by Francesca Giuliani-Hoffman, *CNN*

No, I don't have anything original to say; whatever made you think that? Like many would-be authors, I was struggling to find my voice until the glorious day dawned when I realised I didn't have one. In that liberating moment, I invented a whole new genre: Literary Minimalism. After all, if John Cage can compose four minutes and thirty-three seconds of silence (the original score to which has been lost, of course), and Robert Ryman's white-on-white painting can fetch $15 million at auction, surely there must be a place for minimalism in literature.

You won't have read it, but *Stories I Never Wrote* was one of my early works. It wasn't published in an anthology of the same name and overnight brought me almost no recognition in literary circles. I went from being just another aspiring author to a superstar nonentity. I followed that one with my autobiography, which I called *I Didn't Write This One Either*, and a slim volume entitled *The Wit and Wisdom of Donald Trump*, but that one got censored.

It's not easy being a writer.

Andrew Ball's Biography

After a career doing something else, Andrew Ball now raises Black Angus cattle on the banks of the Rappahannock River in Tidewater, Virginia, an occupation that leaves his mind free to wander. Occasionally, those wanderings turn themselves into stories.

93: SEVEN BLASTS GO VIRAL

by Andrew Carter

Inspired by: "Seven of Donald Trump's most misleading coronavirus claims" by Oliver Milman, *The Guardian, Australian Edition*

"Nobody knew there would be a pandemic or epidemic of this proportion," blasts Uniquehorn.

Obama's administration drew up 69 pages on fighting pandemics until Uniquehorn threw it into the fire, "You're fired."

"It's like a miracle – it will disappear."

Australia, the Amazon and California burn.

"Anybody that needs a test gets a test. We – they're there. They have the tests. And the tests are beautiful," claims Uniquehorn. "It's totally under control."

A star falls, burning one-third of the Earth.

"I've always known this is a real – this is a pandemic. I felt it was a pandemic long before it was called a pandemic. I've always viewed it as very serious."

Earth becomes darkness.

"Americans will have access to vaccines, I think, relatively soon."

Woe no.

"I don't think it's hoarding, I think it's maybe worse than hoarding. But check it out."

Hospitals deal with multiplying cases and locusts plague Earth.

"You can call it a flu, you can call it a virus, you know you can call it many different names."

Let's make America hate again.

Andrew Carter's Biography

Andrew has been published in news and magazines including: *Cairns Post*, *Australian National Library*, *Raconteur* and a poetry competition where he placed second out of three entries, (first and third went to children). He likes fishing, gardening, beer and comedy.

Twitter: @andysea4

94: HIDDEN BEAUTY

by Meghan O'Brien

Inspired by: "Strippers back, but keeping their masks on" by Kevin Connor, *Toronto Sun*

A slow, cool sweat crept its way through the three-layer mask Corine was wearing. The edict had been simple enough in what felt like eons ago:

'Leave your mask on when you leave the house and fewer people will die.'

It was just so unfortunate that she finally had beautiful teeth and no one to smile them at. All covered up, her expensive beauty faded into a sea of anonymity. A wash of faceless facemask-blue forced her to blend in wearing her own.

Sure, a few folks were crafty enough to show off their floral prints or team logos, but Corine was no good with a needle, especially not the kind junkies employed. She herself, occasionally during those younger years, had only ever dabbled in a few bumps of nose candy. Ironically, it was the real type of candy, sugary sweet Cadbury's, that had forced her to buy those new teeth.

Out loud, she laughed, feeling a bit silly that, in a few minutes, the mask would be the only thing she wore while at the gentleman's club.

Meghan O'Brien's Biography

Meghan O'Brien is an upstate New York native who enjoys writing, horseback riding, cooking and gaming. She and her husband reside along the Mohawk River with their three cats.

95: RISING BASKET WOVEN

by Duane L. Herrmann

Inspired by: "Papua New Guinea: House of Worship takes shape" by Anonymous, *Bahá'í World News Service*

Like an upturned woven basket, it will sit on top of a hill in the capital city, just now coming into view. When completed, it will be open to all with no separation, no alienation. It will be a place of worship, unique in the world and the first in the country.

This House of Worship will have no altar, no images, no preaching, no priests, no collection of money – not in this religion.

The design of a woven basket is deliberate to be a point of unity for the 800-plus tribes of native people in this land, each with their own distinct language. How to bridge that gap? And, just two generations or so ago, the tribes were warring and eating each other. Now the tribesmen are airline mechanics, stewardesses and pilots. And hold many other current occupations too.

The country has advanced from the stone age to the space age in less than a century and this unique building is part of that advancement. This is the Bahá'í House of Worship rising in Port Moresby, Papua New Guinea.

Duane L. Herrmann's Biography

Duane L Herrmann survived an abusive childhood embellished with dyslexia, ADHD and now cyclothymia and PTSD. He knows whereof he writes. He grew up and remains on the Kansas prairie where breeze and trees calm him and help him write.

96: THE STOWAWAYS

by Yvonne Mastaglio

Inspired by: "Last-minute change lets you buy a Christmas tree" by Anonymous, *The Times*

"Brenda," Bernard shouted. "Heard the latest news? Humans can buy Christmas trees early this year due to the virus."

Good news for this beetle family with their nine mini-beetles. In the forest, the family all clung to the fir tree while it was being felled. Once down, the tree was encased in plastic and loaded on the roof of a car. Shaking during the bumpy journey, the beetles clung to the branches. Arriving at the tall terraced house, the tree was put in a red ceramic pot in the huge bay window for the world to see. Excited children decorated the tree.

Brenda saw an opportunity when a Santa house was placed on the tree. An ideal home for her and Bernard and the mini-beetles. Oh, how they enjoyed five weeks in their new home until disaster struck when the tree became mangled in the council's garden recycling wagon.

Yvonne Mastaglio's Biography

Married to Paul. Have a lovely cat, Toby. Do archery, skiing. Enjoy walking, reading and was a ballerina in my younger days.

97: THE TROUBLE WITH OUTSOURCING

by Stephen P. Thompson

Inspired by: "US employee 'outsourced job to China'" by Anonymous, *BBC*

I didn't want to go and sit through yet another boring conference, pretending to be interested in the latest developments, schmoozing with wannabes and greasy pole climbers. But it's part of the job. How could I get out of it?

Then it struck me: I didn't have to get out of it. I just didn't actually have to go. I could pay someone to go for me. Then it dawned, I could pay someone to be me, I could hire an actor. I would write the speech, they would deliver it. The advantages were obvious, suave film star looks, relaxed slick delivery, full of easy charm and red carpet style, but with just a hint of bad boy perhaps. They could even do the small talk schmooze. How could I possibly loose?

Well, actors are expensive, or at least decent ones. So I opted for a lookalike, someone who looks like a film star. To be more precise, I hired a Johnny Depp lookalike.

How was I to know he would show up seemingly drunk and dressed as a pirate?

Stephen P. Thompson's Biography

I am a scientist, musician, songwriter and author, searching for the origins of life and our world in science, the meaning of life in fiction and its pointlessness in music. My current contribution addresses none of these worthy subjects.

98: WHY THE MONOLITHS CAME

by Sarah Charmley

Inspired by: "Monolith now spotted in Isle of Wight – the fourth monolith appears in the UK" by Sean Martin, *Express*

It's a strange way to communicate with people. What is it saying? Why has it appeared there? The media goes mad.

Is it a prank? Or a mystery to solve – call Scooby Doo and the gang now.

Or an experiment...

"I told you not to press that button," said Oroak.

I had the wisdom to look chastened. Regret is not an emotion familiar to me. It is easier to say sorry than ask permission and all that.

"Now, look what you have done – you have drawn attention and that may mean discovery of our Earth base."

"I am sure the fuss will die down," I offered. "The pandemic will switch their attention soon."

He tapped his foreclaw on the dash – a warning sign to ignore at your peril.

"This will have to go higher. You cannot show our communications array to the humans. You will expose us."

A shrug.

I am now in the brig, awaiting trial. The judge will be prejudiced, the sentence death by instant dissolve.

The moral: never discover what that button does by pressing it – ask.

VOLUME 1

Sarah Charmley's Biography

Freelance writer, editor, proofreader and storyteller, keeper of hamsters and guinea pigs, singer and puppeteer. Lives in Worcestershire, UK.
www.linkedin.com/in/sarah-charmley/

99: STRAIGHT 9S

by Brian Mackinney

Inspired by: "Now schools set their OWN exams: Head teachers prepare to hold mock tests so pupils can have robust grades while some students could still sit international GCSEs – as 92% of teachers say Gavin Williamson should resign" by Martin Robinson, *Mail Online*

She had always been top of the class right from reception. June could read before she went to school and had a head start. She knew her phonics by the time she was 5.

SATs at the end of Key Stage 2 destroyed her reputation as Exam Phobia took over. Her predicted grades of 5 and even 6 came in at 3 and 4.

By the time she reached Year 11, and with GCSEs looming, her confidence was shattering. June was saved by the school's COVID policy that allowed her to choose her own method of assessment. Faith restored.

Brian Mackinney's Biography

Brian Mackinney is an eighty year old drabble writer whose drabbles can be found on:
www.clivef9.wixsite.com/macdrabble-tales

100: CLASSROOM VS. ONLINE CLASSES: WHICH ONE IS THE MORE EFFECTIVE WAY TO LEARN?

by Mehak Vijay Chawla

Inspired by: "Virtual Vs Real: Online learning is better than in-person education" by Himanshi Upadhaya, *Hindustan Times*

The classroom environment is one of the most important factors affecting student learning. Students learn better when they view the learning environment as positive and supportive.

The classroom environment is essential to promote and stimulate collaborative learning. Collaborative learning increases a student's self-awareness about how other students learn and enables them to learn more easily and effectively, transforming them into keen learners inside and beyond the classroom. It gives an excellent opportunity to build organisational skills.

Although students save time and money by learning online, with the ability to study anywhere, online learners can complete coursework at home, at a coffee shop or a library. This advantage allows students to work in the environment that best suits them. Learning online can help students hone the technical skills they need for a job.

At last, online classes are important in a coronavirus pandemic situation, which we are facing today all over the world. So, online education is the most effective way of learning in this pandemic, but we all miss our classrooms a lot.

Mehak Vijay Chawla's Biography

I am a published poet (anthology) from New Delhi, India, studying in secondary school. I am most happy when I am singing, doing cubism art, trying new fonts of calligraphy. I hope to be a famous young poet, artist.
 Instagram:@mehakkvc

VOLUME 1

A FINAL NOTE

Alice and I would like to say one last THANK YOU to all the authors featured in this anthology. Their generosity is helping support a very worthy charity and it's an honour to present their stories in this collection.

Don't forget to check my website for more writing challenges. You will be able to find all the details here: www.christopherfielden.com/writing-challenges/

There is also an 'Authors of the Flash Fiction Writing Challenges' Facebook group that runs its own regular challenges. It's open to everyone. Please feel free to join here:
www.facebook.com/groups/157928995061095/

I will say farewell Bristol-style:

Cheers me dears,

Chris Fielden

Printed in Great Britain
by Amazon